THE *Jessie* FILES

A BOXCAR CHILDREN BOOK

Talk of the Town

Book 2

THE *Jessie* FILES

A BOXCAR CHILDREN BOOK

Talk of the Town

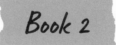

Book 2

Stacia Deutsch

Based on Characters Created by Gertrude Chandler Warner

Albert Whitman & Company
Chicago, Illinois

Library of Congress Cataloging-in-Publication data
is on file with the publisher.

Text copyright © 2022 by Albert Whitman & Company
First published in the United States of America in 2022
by Albert Whitman & Company
ISBN 978-0-8075-3788-6 (hardcover)
ISBN 978-0-8075-3789-3 (ebook)

THE BOXCAR CHILDREN® is a registered trademark
of Albert Whitman & Company.

Printed in the United States of America
10 9 8 7 6 5 4 3 2 1 LB 26 25 24 23 22

Jacket art copyright © 2022 by Albert Whitman & Company
Jacket art by Mina Price
Design by Aphelandra
Chapter opener graphic sourced from Vecteezy (@doraclub)

The Boxcar Children® created by Gertrude Chandler Warner

Visit The Boxcar Children® online at www.boxcarchildren.com.
For more information about Albert Whitman & Company,
visit our website at www.albertwhitman.com.

Gratitude to Fred and Pat Hedenberg
for their dedication to the Boxcar Children's past
and to Laura, Ana, and Lydia Sebastian
for helping me shape the future

Contents

Chapter 1

Glitch in the System

"You have the coolest cat in the world," I told my best friend, Charla. Pippen was curled up next to me on Charla's bed. His fuzzy, white face was adorable. It was extra cute that he snored lightly while he snoozed. "Watch is still my favorite animal overall, but Pippen is my favorite cat."

Charla laughed. "Your dog's pretty awesome, Jessie." Pippen raised his head for a second and stared at Charla. "Don't get jealous," she told him. "You know I'll always love you best." Pippen purred.

I took the green ribbon out of my hair and dangled it in front of Pippen. He began to bat the fabric around with his paw. "I think he listens to everything we say."

"I know, right?" Charla pointed to her computer screen. "I'm going to submit a video of him to this website." For the last hour, Charla had been sitting at her desk and surfing the internet while I finished up a little homework. "I love this site," she said. "It shows you a few quick videos, then you vote for which ones show the smartest cats in Greenfield."

I took back my ribbon and tied it neatly around my hair. Pippen started to protest, then quickly decided to go back to sleep instead.

Charla said, "You could post a video of Watch for their smartest dogs list. There are also smart horses, smart goats..." She stopped scrolling. "Oh, and look, there's even a list of the smartest people in Greenfield posted here. No videos though."

"Smart people, eh? Am I on it?" I chuckled before getting off the bed to look over Charla's shoulder.

I noticed Charla's new glasses sitting on the desk. She was supposed to use them all the time, but I rarely saw her wear them. I pointed at the glasses, and she put them on, blinked hard, then took them off again and set them back on the desk. I didn't wear glasses, but I'd heard that new lenses could be hard to get used to.

"Sorry. You're not on the list," she said, squinting at the page. "But if they knew how smart you are, Jessie, I'm sure they'd happily include you." Charla laughed. "And Daniel too, of course."

Daniel was the third member of our Three Musketeers friend group. The three musketeers were swashbuckling characters from an old book. They always had each other's backs. We were a lot like that, even though I don't think any of us had ever been in a sword fight.

After Charla started calling us the Three Musketeers, I read the book. It was written more than 150 years ago, and it turns out there were really four friends in the story. I don't know why it wasn't called *The Four Musketeers*. In the story, the musketeers used the motto "All for one and one for all." That had become our motto too.

Just a few weeks earlier, the three of us had worked together to solve a mystery in town. I hadn't wanted to be a detective anymore. I had already done plenty of that alongside my sister and brothers from the boxcar that served as our home base. I was in middle school now and ready for something new, but Daniel and Charla had convinced me to help them with an investigation. Pretty quickly, I realized that I actually didn't mind solving mysteries as long as my friends were on the case too. We were always going to be all for one and one for all.

"You should add yourself to the smartest people list," I told Charla. At the beginning of the year, she had joined the coding club at school. I didn't know anyone who could figure out computer stuff as fast as she could.

"Me? No way. But I *am* officially making a submission right now," Charla said. "I've been doing research on some of history's greatest computer programmers. I think Clarisse Potter should be the top choice for this list." She said, "Dr. Potter was so smart that she had two PhDs. If one PhD makes you a doctor, does two make you a doctor-doctor?"

"If you have two PhDs, you can probably call yourself whatever you want," I said. Then, because I didn't know anything about Clarisse Potter, I asked, "When did Dr. Potter die?"

Charla spun her chair around and lowered her dark eyes at me. "How did you know she died?" she asked.

"I figured it out because you talked about her in the past tense," I said.

"Oh, right," Charla said, her serious expression instantly turning into a bright smile. "Good observation as always, Jessie." She spun back to face the computer screen. "Dr. Potter died three months ago in a car accident." Charla sighed. "I was really sad when I heard the news. I always wanted to meet her, and now I never will."

I plopped myself down in a beanbag chair next to Charla's desk. "Tell me more."

Charla clicked a tab at the top of her browser. The image of a very stylish older woman filled the screen. She was about sixty, and she had short, rainbow-dyed hair and big, chunky earrings. Her black tank top revealed a tattoo high on her right shoulder.

"Is that a maze?" I asked, staring at the inked lines and dots.

"It's a circuit board," Charla said. She pointed at her own T-shirt, which had a similar design on the front. Charla had Greenfield's best collection of computer-themed T-shirts.

Judging from the photo, I would have guessed that Clarisse Potter was a rock star, not a computer programmer.

"You're looking at one of the most important women in programming," Charla said. "Clarisse Potter developed some of the world's strongest cybersecurity systems."

I knew that meant she created tools to protect computers. "Dr. Potter was from Greenfield?" I asked.

"How do you not know this already? She lived just outside town in a huge old house," Charla replied. She loaded up another website. "I've been reading all about her because my mom is representing her children in a lawsuit." Charla's mom was a lawyer.

I looked at the site Charla had just pulled up. There was a photo of two people, both about forty years old, standing in front of a historic stone manor. I read the bold print above the picture: "Leona and Gideon Potter Strive to Honor Their Mother's Legacy." I scanned the article.

"That headline is misleading," I said, wrinkling my nose. "Their lawsuit isn't really about honoring Dr. Potter. It says that they are looking to keep control of her work. It doesn't say they're opening a museum or donating the materials to the university in her honor."

In newspaper club, we'd been working on ways to write a headline that truly expressed what was in the article. I began thinking about how I would rewrite this one when Charla's mom stepped into the room.

"Didn't mean to eavesdrop, but you girls are rather loud," Mrs. Gray said. She explained some of the details of the lawsuit. "Dr. Potter had an assistant named Gloria Scott. Ms. Scott is also a talented programmer, and it seems she considers herself the right person to carry on Dr. Potter's legacy. After the car accident, she took piles of Dr. Potter's notes and journals home."

I'd never seen Mrs. Gray look so tired. As usual, her hair was tightly pulled back, but messy strands had escaped and were sticking out at odd angles. Mrs. Gray rubbed her red-rimmed eyes. For a moment, I thought she might be about to curl up with Pippen on the bed.

Instead, she yawned and said, "When someone dies,

you can't just take their stuff. That's illegal. I'm trying to force Ms. Scott to give everything back to the family."

"Mom, you gotta get some sleep," Charla said. There was a worried tone in her voice.

"Gideon and Leona emailed me some new video evidence for the trial," Mrs. Gray responded. "I downloaded the file, but you're right. I'm just too tired to deal with it right now. I'll get a fresh start tomorrow."

I looked out the window. It wasn't completely dark yet, but we had school the next day. The weekend was almost over.

"I should go," I said. "It's almost time for the bedtime story." Every Sunday night, I read to my younger brother, Benny, and my sister, Violet, before we all went to sleep. My older brother, Henry, usually came to listen too.

Mrs. Gray stretched her arms and yawned. "I'll go change into pj's. Charla, honey, can you do me a favor?"

"Sure, Mom," Charla said.

She pointed toward the living room. "My laptop's on the table. Would you mind shutting it down and plugging it in for the night?"

"No problem," Charla said as her mom kissed her forehead. "When does Dad get back?"

Charla's dad traveled for his job and wasn't around a lot. In all the time I'd known Charla, I'd only met him a couple of times.

"Next week," Mrs. Gray said as she yawned again.

I followed Charla into the living room and sat next to her on the comfy leather couch. Charla opened her mom's laptop.

"You should write an article about the lawsuit for the *Greenfield Gabber*," she told me.

I was a feature writer, which basically meant I could write about anything I wanted as long as it connected to school somehow. What did a lawsuit have to do with our school?

"I don't think I can," I began, but the truth was that I wanted to find out more. Not just about the case, but about Clarisse Potter herself. She sounded (and looked) amazing. "Do you think Clarisse went to Greenfield Middle School?" I asked Charla. "That would give me an angle."

"Should be easy to find out." Charla clicked on a search bar instead of shutting down the laptop. Just as she was typing Clarisse's name, Charla's cell phone buzzed. She pulled it from her pants pocket.

"Message from Daniel," Charla told me. "It says 'check your email.'" She began to open her email app when the phone screen suddenly blacked out. "Ack. My phone just shut down—battery died." Her fingers flew over her mom's computer keys. "Oh well. I'll just open the email here." A second later, Daniel's video message appeared on the laptop's screen.

"I've decided to try out for the school play," Daniel began. He brushed his brown hair from his eyes. "Wanted you to see my audition first."

"I can't believe it!" I gushed. Our friend Daniel was super shy at school. He barely talked. But with me and Charla, Daniel was completely different. "If he's really gotten over his shyness, he'll be a perfect fit for the theater club."

"Let's see the audition." Charla turned up the computer's volume.

In the video, Daniel was wearing a tight green shirt and matching shorts. He was a great artist, and he'd used his skills to paint his face green with brownish warts.

"Check it out! He's Hop-Man!" Charla cheered, recognizing the costume of her favorite comic book superhero. I'd read a couple comics and thought the half-man, half-frog hero was funny, but I wasn't a mega-fan like Charla and Daniel. They were obsessed.

"What do you call a sad frog?" Daniel croaked.

"That's a line from the newest issue!" Charla exclaimed. "It was just released."

At the same time, she and Daniel shouted, "Unhoppy!"

Daniel began hopping around the video frame, shouting, "Hop away!" which was the superhero's catch-phrase. He bounced into the walls and crawled on the carpet. He rolled around, pretending to capture a villain with his sticky tongue.

Charla and I couldn't stop laughing as we watched Daniel in action.

At the end, Daniel stood up and wiped the paint off his face with a towel. He looked into the camera and said, "Just messing with you!" He laughed. "I mean, I'm serious about trying out, but I'm not going to do it as Hop-Man." With that, he waved at the camera and said, "See you at school!"

"You have to send that to me!" I begged Charla. "Daniel probably sent it to you because of your Hop-Man bond." Part of me wished he'd thought to send it to me too, but I understood.

"I'm sure he wouldn't mind," Charla said. She attached the video file to an email and started typing my address. As she did, something strange happened. First, the computer screen went black. Then, the screen flashed back on and the cursor began to move around in jumps and jitters. Charla tried to get control, but the cursor bounced randomly around the screen.

Her email whooshed away even though Charla never pressed send.

After all that, the screen flashed black again before everything settled back to normal.

"What just happened?" I asked, staring at the computer.

"I have no idea," Charla admitted, looking just as surprised as I felt. She closed out of the browser. "I'm sure there's a logical explanation though. The computer's probably just overheated from my mom using it all day. We'll let it rest and I'll check with her about it in the morning." Charla shut everything down and plugged the laptop in, just like her mom had asked.

I slipped on my favorite striped sweater. It was a hand-me-down from Henry, and I wore it a lot. The weather was getting cooler, and soon I'd need a jacket, but not tonight.

Charla walked me to her apartment door.

"I'm so happy Daniel's trying out for the play," I said. "Too bad there isn't a Hop-Man story for the stage. He could be a star."

"You're a writer," Charla said. "You should write one."

I gave her a not-in-a-million-years look, and we both laughed.

After saying goodbye, I walked into the cool night feeling warm inside. Things with my best friend were going well. Daniel was coming out of his shell. And I just maybe had a lead on a new story for the *Greenfield Gabber*.

Things were headed in the right direction.

Chapter 2

Digital Disaster

When I walked into art class the next morning, I knew something was wrong right away. Mr. Masoud wasn't there yet, but Charla and Daniel were already in their seats. They weren't talking to each other in the middle of the room like they normally would. Instead, they were both staring straight ahead like they were trying to avoid making eye contact.

"What's up?" I asked Charla. My seat was next to hers at the front of the class, while Daniel always sat in the back.

She shrugged. "Nothing. Why?"

"Uh, you said a new issue of Hop-Man came out," I said. "Normally you and Daniel would be yammering on and on about stuff that only makes sense to…well, you and Daniel."

She shrugged again, as if she didn't really want to talk to me. I took the hint and hurried back to see Daniel. On the way, I noticed a couple kids come into the classroom. They were both holding their phones and laughing at whatever was on the screen.

"Did I do something wrong?" I asked Daniel. "Is Charla mad at me?"

Just like Charla, Daniel only shrugged at me. Then he flopped his head down on his desk with a small clunk.

Two more kids came into the room. As they passed by, one of the boys croaked like a frog.

"Daniel the Tadpole," the other said. They started laughing and high-fived each other.

"Daniel?" I asked. "What's going on?"

"Ask Charla," he muttered without raising his head off the desk.

More kids came into the room, and just about all of them seemed to be in on some kind of joke.

I went back to Charla. "I don't understand," I said. I repeated the question: "What's going on?"

She stared at me with darts in her eyes. "Why did you send Daniel's video to the whole school?"

"I—what—huh?"

Mr. Masoud entered the room. "Phones away," he said. "Today we're drawing self-portraits."

At that, the laughter stopped and everyone got busy. I couldn't focus on my art, and my self-portrait came out like a big tomato with brown ponytails. I even spelled my name wrong when I signed the bottom of the paper.

When the bell finally rang, I blocked Charla's way to the door. "Seriously, please talk to me," I said.

She was so mad she didn't look at me as she spoke. "You're the only person I sent Daniel's video to. Now everyone has it." She put her hands on her hips. "It doesn't take a detective to figure out who shared the video."

It didn't take long for what she was saying to sink in. Someone had spread Daniel's Hop-Man video all around school. And Charla thought I was the one who did it.

"You really think I would do that?" I asked. "Are you serious? I never even got your email."

"If you didn't do it, then who did?" Charla's eyes narrowed.

"I don't know," I said. It seemed like everyone else knew more about what was going on than I did.

Charla huffed and began to walk away. Then after a few steps, she stopped. "I don't want to fight," she said with a sigh.

"I don't want to either. But I really didn't send the video." We stood in the hallway as the second-period students filed into the art room.

"Sorry," Charla said, her voice soft. "I shouldn't have blamed you."

"It's okay. I get it," I told her. I felt awful that Daniel's video was public. "Daniel hates attention, and now everyone is looking at him."

"We can't take the video back," Charla told me. "Someone put it online, and it's basically impossible to get anything off the internet once it's there. But maybe if we figure out how this happened, we can make it up to Daniel." Her voice trailed off before she added, "Somehow."

I tried, but I couldn't think of anything that might make Daniel feel better. Last time we were all in an argument, I'd baked cookies. I doubted chocolate chips would make his embarrassment go away though.

"Meet me in the computer lab at lunch," Charla said. "We might not take back the video, but maybe we can help him be a little less mad."

Daniel had only sent that video to Charla, and she forwarded it to me. Now everyone had seen it. He was right to be angry at us. My heart hurt from thinking that it might take time before we were the Three Musketeers again.

I looked around the hallway. Daniel was nowhere in sight.

"Less mad sounds like a good place to start," I said. "See you at noon."

We both hurried off to our next class.

∘ ∘ ∘

Charla was already tapping on a keyboard when I entered the computer lab. The lab was always open to students, but I only ever visited with my classes. For Charla, it was like a second homeroom. The coding club met there, and she'd often stop in between classes to work on a project or to look up random things.

"I'm logging into my mom's email account first so I can check something," Charla told me. "Grab a seat."

I was so tense and sad about our problems with Daniel that I didn't feel like sitting. While Charla logged in as her mom, I paced around. Walking didn't make me feel any better though, so I tried counting the computers. That didn't help either.

Grandfather always said that people can soak up sadness just like a sponge soaks up water—and it can be super hard to wring out. I definitely felt heavy and soggy inside.

"I keep warning my mom," Charla muttered. "You'd think she'd understand. But nooooo. It's just too easy."

"What are you mumbling?" I asked from across the room.

"My mom has the simplest password for her computer and uses the same one for her email," Charla explained. "You'd think since she's representing the Potter family, she'd know something about cyber-security." Charla shook a fist at the computer and exclaimed, "Pippen12345 is NOT secure!"

At that, she quickly looked around to make sure no one had overheard the password. We were the only ones in the room. "The name of our cat is in her bio on the law firm website. There's a photo of him on her key-chain. *And* she has an 'I heart Pippen' sticker on the car!"

"Your mom likes the cat," I said. "It's a great honor to be a named in a password." I thought I was being funny, but Charla didn't laugh.

She groaned. "I keep warning Mom that if she doesn't change it to something more random, something ugly will eventually happen." Charla scanned the screen and exhaled slowly. "Looks like Mom got lucky," she said. "I'm not seeing anything that pops out as unusual."

She logged out of her mom's account and opened her own email.

"Oh no!" Charla shouted. "Jessie, this is bad. Very, very bad!"

I hurried across the room.

Again, Charla asked me to sit down. This time I did, but on the edge of the seat. My legs kept shaking, and I couldn't seem to relax no matter how hard I tried.

Charla showed me an email in her sent items. On the line where she was supposed to write my email address, it said "GreenfieldMiddleCodingClub."

"Is that a group name?" I asked. We had a similar one for everyone at the *Gabber* called "Greenfield-MiddleNewspaperClub."

"Ugh, this is terrible," Charla groaned. "It was me after all! It was an accident, but I'm the one who sent Daniel's video to the entire coding club email list."

"And the coders sent it to their friends?" I asked.

"They must have," she said. Now her knees were jittery too. "And those people sent it to their other friends, and so on…"

"Until the video was all over school." I sighed. This really was terrible.

"It's my fault," Charla said. Her shoulders slumped as she let go of all the air in her body.

"The email went out from your account, but I don't think it's actually your fault at all," I told her. As I stood up, I felt more steady, and my head started to clear. "You didn't put the group in the addressees." Charla glanced back at me. "Remember?" I asked her. "The computer was glitching out."

"Still," Charla said. "I should have done more to keep the video safe." Her voice cracked. "Daniel will never forgive me."

"He will," I assured her, suddenly feeling very confident. "In another day or two, this will all blow over. Everyone will be talking about something else."

"Maybe," Charla said. She logged out of her email. "But in the meantime, I need to go find Daniel. I have to explain."

"Wait." I stopped her from leaving the room. "I think he needs more time by himself."

When my sister, Violet, was upset about something, she liked to hole up in her room for "processing." It meant she wanted to be left alone for a while. I was more of a talk-it-out kind of person, but I had to respect that everyone had their own way of dealing with emotions. The way Daniel flopped his head down on his desk in art class and avoided me reminded me of

Violet. He'd made it clear he wasn't ready to talk about the situation.

"I don't know." Charla got up and began to pace. "The guilt feels like a rock in my belly."

"We'll explain it to him tomorrow," I assured her. "You have coding club this afternoon. I have the newspaper. Daniel has art time with Mr. Masoud." Mondays were busy at school. "He probably wants to go home after all that. He can hang out with his family and shake off the day." That's what Violet would do if something similar happened to her.

Charla looked uncertain but agreed to be patient.

We were about to go back to the cafeteria for a fast lunch when Charla's phone buzzed. She read the message.

"It's my mom," said Charla. "She wants to know if I saw the file from the Potter case in her email or on the desktop."

"The video evidence that she said came in last night?" I asked. We hadn't looked at Charla's mom's messages. We'd only watched Daniel's video. Then there was the glitch, and Charla had shut the laptop down.

Charla tapped a quick message back to her mom.

"The file she needs is missing," Charla reported after a few seconds. "No sign of it anywhere."

That was strange. "Could someone take the email back after they sent it?" I asked somewhat hopefully.

"No." Charla explained, "Once you hit send, the message goes to someone else's email server. You can't get it back." She added, "My mom had already gotten it for sure. Plus, she'd downloaded a copy of the video file to her own hard drive."

Charla sent a text to her mom and waited for the reply.

"Mom is going to talk to Leona and Gideon Potter this afternoon," Charla reported. She looked at me. "She wants us to come along and explain what happened."

"I don't know, Charla," I said. "I don't want to miss club time." Newspaper deadlines came fast, and Ms. Surovsky expected the writers to be at every meeting.

"This is important, Jessie," Charla told me. It was so quiet in the room that I could hear my heart beating when Charla said, "I think my mom's been hacked."

Chapter 3

Hacker on the Loose

After school, Charla and I rode our bikes to Potter Manor. Ms. Surovsky hadn't been thrilled that I was missing the meeting, but it was nice to get away from school after all the drama with Daniel.

"I can't believe Clarisse Potter lived this close to us the whole time," Charla said as we rounded a corner. The house was only a couple of miles away, but it was up a big hill. "I could have met her!"

"Maybe you did," I said, huffing and puffing as we pedaled. "You both might have been at the grocery store or the ice cream parlor at the same time."

"Wouldn't that be amazing?" Charla gushed. She took a big breath and rushed her words. "I'm going to try facial recognition on my photo software tonight and see if she's in the background of any of my pictures."

This is one of the things I admired about Charla. If she could use technology to figure something out, she would do it. I'd never have thought to scan my entire photo library, but as we rode on in silence, I knew she was already figuring out the details of how to put her idea into action.

"I hope I met her," Charla said, pumping her legs to get up the last crest.

We stopped at a large, modern security gate and got off our bikes. The walls around the manor were made of thick steel bars covered with green ivy. Charla quickly figured out that the plants were being used to hide security cameras. She pointed out a camera lens as she rang the small doorbell under a plaque that said "Potter."

While we waited for someone to talk to us through

a speaker under the plaque, I said, "New shirt?" Her T-shirt today was tie-dyed and had a graphic of an old computer disc, a plus sign, and the letter O. I'd noticed it at school, but I'd forgotten to mention how much I liked the "disc-o" joke.

"The T-shirt shop at the mall is running out of new designs for me," Charla said with a laugh. "So I made my own." She smiled. "This is my first try. I created the design with free software, then printed the iron-on transfer myself." She spun around as if she was modeling the shirt.

"It's really cool," I told her as my breathing returned to normal.

She told me she'd been working on it all week but didn't want to show me until it was done. "I can make you a shirt too, Jessie," Charla said. Since no one had come to greet us yet, she rang the bell on the gate again. "What do you want on it?"

"Maybe we could make something awesome for the *Gabber* staff?" I suggested.

Before we left school, I'd dropped off a note for Ms. Surovsky, saying I'd stop by tomorrow to talk about my next feature. I hoped that while I was at the manor today, I'd find a connection between Clarisse Potter and the school so I could pitch an article about her.

"Maybe I should make shirts for coding club too," Charla said thoughtfully. "Although after what happened today, I don't think they deserve one. I still can't believe people shared that video."

"They didn't think it was private," I said. "They thought it was funny." She frowned when I added, "I bet someday Daniel will think it's funny too."

Charla stared through the thick iron bars on the gate and said, "Or maybe someday I'll be a cybersecurity expert. I'll stop hackers so no one accidentally emails embarrassing videos or steals my mom's files."

"Good idea," I said, though I hoped Daniel would come around long before Charla became a cybersecurity expert.

Charla raised her finger to ring the bell one more time, and the gate suddenly began to slide open. A voice through the intercom said, "Leave your bicycles by the tree and wipe your shoes on the mat before entering the house."

"Thanks, Mom," Charla said, recognizing the voice. She turned to me. "Mom hates dirty shoes in the house."

"I know." Whenever I'd visited Charla's place, there was always a neat line of shoes by the front door. No one had to explain it. I always took off my shoes and added them to the line before entering the apartment.

Potter Manor was not at all like I imagined. The gate and fence were super modern and decked out with high-tech camera equipment, but the house was old and even a bit run-down. A big tree grew in the center of a grassy yard. Red and yellow leaves were piled up on the lawn, raked and ready to be bagged.

We leaned our bikes against the thick tree trunk and were about to head to the house when the roar of an engine caught my attention. I looked across the yard and noticed a person leaning over a lawn mower.

"Don't we know that boy?" Charla asked me. She'd forgotten her glasses today. Again. Squinting into the distance, she said, "He seems kinda familiar."

"Tall. Skinny. Dark hair." I put the clues together before he turned to face us. "It's Milo Miller." Milo played football for Greenfield Middle School, and I knew he'd been selected to play on a citywide team as well. His picture had been in the last edition of the *Gabber*.

Milo waved. We waved back.

"He always seems nice, even though most of his friends are annoying," Charla said as we climbed the crumbling stone steps to the manor door. She added, "I don't know him very well, but he hangs out with that group of guys who act like they have more muscles than brains."

I knew the guys. They all played sports, and that's all they ever talked about. Milo's friend JJ Stewart was in the newspaper club and had the beat of reporting scores and game highlights. Milo and the others came by the newspaper office sometimes to review the details of the games. Ms. Surovsky usually told them they were being too loud and made them leave.

I let the sound of the lawn mower fade to the back of my mind as Charla's mom opened the manor door.

Mrs. Gray waited for us to wipe our feet on a rough woven mat before leading us down the hallway. "I'm glad you both could come." As we walked alongside her, Mrs. Gray said, "Charla, I'll need you to explain any computer-related details that I might miss, okay?"

Charla nodded.

"It's good to have your eyes and ears on this as well, Jessie," Mrs. Gray continued. "We all know how good you are at spotting the details no one else notices." She opened a creaky door and escorted us into a large parlor.

The room was barely decorated. No art or photos hung on the walls, but there was a big bay window overlooking the lawn and the tree. I noticed Milo was out there, bagging the brightly colored leaves.

Toward the center of the room, two couches faced each other with a low wooden table sitting between them. One couch was bright yellow and looked brand-new. The other was a dull, faded shade of red and looked as if it had seen a lot of use over the years.

Several books by Clarisse Potter were displayed on the table. A framed copy of the photo Charla had shown me online was on display between the stacked hardbacks. It seemed like Clarisse was staring out from the photo, watching us and wondering what we were doing in her house.

Mrs. Gray straightened her dark blue suit jacket before introducing me and Charla to Leona and Gideon Potter, who were sitting on the yellow sofa. I recognized them from the photo I'd seen on Charla's computer.

"It's a bit unusual for a lawyer to bring along her daughter, isn't it?" Gideon raised one eyebrow as he asked the question. His blue eyes darted from me to Charla as we sat down alongside Mrs. Gray on the dull-red couch. "And her friend as well," he added.

"It's always good to have another set of eyes and ears," Mrs. Gray said, repeating what she'd told me in the hallway. "Think of Charla and Jessie as my assistants." Mrs. Gray's hair was slicked back, and not a strand was out of place today. She looked tough, no-nonsense, and very professional.

Leona didn't appear to care one way or another if we were there. She seemed to only have one thing on her mind. "Let's get to it," she stated. "What can we do to show Ms. Scott that we are serious about getting our mother's work back?"

If I'd seen these two on the street, I'd never have thought them to be brother and sister. Gideon's eyes were blue, while Leona's were green. His hair was so blond it looked white, but hers was almost black.

It looked like they'd gotten dressed up for this meeting. He wore a business suit. She wore a pretty sweater and black pants. I rarely worried too much about my own clothes, but I wished that I'd tried a little harder to get my outfit right today. The long top and leggings I'd worn to school seemed too casual. I glanced at Charla in her colorful T-shirt. She didn't seem to notice what anyone else was wearing. She was 100 percent focused on the conversation.

"I don't know why Gloria is causing so much trouble," Gideon said, his expression hard. "The family has been very generous to her over the years."

Leona looked at Charla and I as she began to explain. "Gloria Scott began her career as a...*hacker*." The way she said "hacker" made it sound despicable, like the worst thing anyone could be.

"Mother discovered Gloria when she successfully hacked her way into the extremely well-protected private network here at the house," Gideon put in. There was something strained in his voice that mirrored his sister's harsh tone.

"She didn't have any formal training," Leona continued, tag-teaming her brother with the storytelling.

He said, "Mother was so impressed with Gloria's skills that she asked her to be part of the Potter Mentorship Program, even though she'd never actually applied."

I heard Charla's breath catch at the mention of the Potter Mentorship Program. I knew she was wondering if the family was going to continue the program now that Dr. Potter was gone. If so, Charla would definitely want to apply.

"Mother said Gloria was the best student she'd ever met," Gideon said. "But I was suspicious from the start. She'd hacked into my own mother's network, and now she was being handed the secrets to her success."

"Hackers hack," Leona said. "That's what they do. They sneak their way inside a computer and mess around."

Charla raised her hand as if she wanted to be called on.

"Do you have something to add?" Mrs. Gray asked.

"Last night, when I was shutting down your laptop, something bugged out." Charla described how the cursor had seemed to move on its own and the screen had gone blank. "It's easy to get access to a laptop if you're good at hacking systems."

"You told me you thought my laptop was hacked," Charla's mom said. "Do you still think that?"

Charla nodded.

"Is it possible to find out who might have done it?" her mom asked.

"Probably not," Charla told her. "But with what we just heard about Gloria Scott, it sounds like she has the skills. And it makes sense, if she wanted to erase that new evidence you received."

Leona nodded in agreement. "As I said before, Gloria Scott is a hacker, and hackers hack."

"I thought of her too at first," said Mrs. Gray. She looked troubled. "Then I looked into her whereabouts last night. Ms. Scott was out to dinner with her father last night. I don't think it could have been her."

"Are you certain?" Leona asked. "It does sound like the sort of thing Ms. Scott would do, given her history."

"Positive," Mrs. Gray said. "The chef at the Downtown Grille is a friend of mine, and she confirmed that Ms. Scott was at the restaurant when my computer was hacked. Not to mention there are reporters following her everywhere these days. This lawsuit is really starting to draw a lot of attention."

As her mom started to discuss the publicity around the case with the Potters, Charla leaned toward me and whispered into my ear, "What do you think? If it wasn't Ms. Scott, who could it have been?"

I considered her question. "If Dr. Potter handpicked Ms. Scott to be her assistant, she's probably a pretty amazing hacker, right?"

"For sure," Charla responded.

"So is it possible she could have hacked your mom's computer even if she wasn't sitting at her own computer at that specific time?" I asked.

"Possibly," Charla whispered to me. "But I'm not

sure how. I guess she could be capable of almost anything though."

"We can't be sure who did it, but important evidence for the Gloria Scott lawsuit was definitely stolen." I looked toward Charla's mom. "And we need to figure out why before things get any worse."

Chapter 4

Evidence Recovered

"There's one more thing that happened last night," Charla told her mom. I could tell Charla wasn't excited to tell her mom what happened with Daniel, but Mrs. Gray needed to know all the information about the security breach. It could be important.

"When the hacker broke into your laptop," Charla continued, "a video of Daniel accidentally got sent to the entire coding club." She described the video and explained how it had gone viral at school.

"Oh dear," Mrs. Gray said. "I'm sorry you got mixed

up in this all." She offered to call Daniel and explain.

"I already apologized," Charla said. "I just thought you should know."

"I don't think any of us can fix Daniel's mood right now," I added. "He needs space."

Charla told her mom, "I want to try to recover the evidence that was deleted from your hard drive."

This would be a big task, but Charla really wanted to give it a go. Maybe all this discussion of world-class programmers like Dr. Potter and Ms. Scott had inspired her to push her own computer skills to the limit.

"That's not necessary," Gideon told Charla. He offered, "I can give you the video footage again. The file we sent you came from the house security cameras."

I decided I needed to stop mentally judging Gideon Potter. When we'd first entered the parlor and he'd asked why Charla and I were there, I'd immediately been suspicious. I was sorry that I'd been so quick to judge. As he stood to lead us from the room, Gideon seemed understanding of the situation, like he wanted to help.

I'd try to be more patient toward Leona too. She was upset, and I shouldn't think badly of her because of that.

"Look to the left." Gideon proudly pointed out a security camera that tracked us as we left the parlor and entered a long, wood-paneled hallway. It was hidden just behind a vase of flowers. Another camera was tucked in a high corner behind a light fixture. As I counted the cameras between where we started and where we were going, I couldn't help but marvel that this house felt more secure than the best museums in the world. It was definitely weird though. The walls were blank and the furniture was old, so I wondered why they needed all this protection. As far as I could tell, there was nothing valuable in the manor except Dr. Potter's computer files.

On my own, I noted a camera that Gideon hadn't pointed out. It was high on the wall at the end of the hallway. Unlike the others, this one was in plain sight. There was a tiny glowing green light at the bottom, which I was pretty sure meant it was currently recording us. I resisted the urge to smile and wave.

We stopped between two closed doors. The door on the left was shut with a simple knob, and there was no lock that I could see. The one on the right looked like something out of a spy movie, with a big metal lock system and a coded keypad. I assumed this lock protected the room where her computer or notes were kept.

"Was Dr. Potter nervous about someone breaking in?" I asked, stepping toward the room on the right. "I've never seen such a serious security system."

"Mother was actually quite trusting," Leona said, reaching for the knob on the left, the one that opened easily.

"Too trusting," Gideon added. "We had the security system and the locks added after her death." He pushed open the door so we could all move inside.

I glanced back at the other door, then to Charla, as we followed them into the room. I didn't understand why the room across the hall was locked so tightly and this one was practically wide open. Neither Gideon nor Leona mentioned what might be stored in the other room.

"Smartest thing we've ever done," Leona added. "Without the cameras, we'd never have seen Gloria breaking into the house." Her voice was frustrated. "We warned Mother about the need for security, but she never listened."

"I feel you," Charla said, tossing a look at her own mother.

"You don't have to keep saying it," Mrs. Gray answered with a slight frown. "Message received, loud and clear. I'll change my passwords tonight." She nudged us forward.

Dr. Potter's computer room had stone walls. Gideon explained that the stones kept the room cool and were fire resistant. They also looked really amazing and made me feel like we were deep underground in some sort of hidden cave. I'd never been in a room like this before.

There were no books or bookcases along the walls. A dramatic spotlight shined down on the center of the room, illuminating Dr. Potter's workspace. The desk was actually a simple beige folding table, just like the one Grandfather had dragged out of the garage for our last yard sale. There were bits and pieces of electronic devices scattered across the table. Amidst the clutter was Dr. Potter's computer setup. It consisted of two wide monitors, a big computer tower, and a plain gray keyboard and mouse. Finally, a big blue rubber ball was tucked under the table.

"Better for posture than a regular chair," Gideon explained as he noticed Charla and I staring at the ball. "Staying balanced requires a tight core." He tapped his abs. "Mom spent so many hours working that she said her chair was her workout." He laughed, low and husky.

I nodded. The ball chair looked fun, but I wasn't sure it would be comfortable for hours of sitting.

I looked around the room again and noticed that Leona had disappeared. I hadn't seen her leave, but now it was only Gideon giving the tour.

Gideon told us, "For security reasons, this room is not connected to the internet or any private networks. It's completely off the grid. Mother kept the data for her most secret projects stored on hard drives in here."

Charla raised her eyebrows and nodded in admiration. A cybersecurity wiz like Dr. Potter knew that the only way to keep a computer completely safe was to keep it offline.

"To get at the data, even a master hacker like Gloria would have to physically enter this room and take the hard drives. And that's just what she tried to do. Lucky for us, she failed. But it's still breaking and entering, even if she didn't get what she came for, right?" He looked at Mrs. Gray as he asked the question.

"Yes," she said in a matter-of-fact way. "Attempted theft is a crime."

"Well, there you have it, then," Gideon said. "If she had the hard drive, along with the notes and journals that she already took, Ms. Scott would have all of Mother's most valuable materials."

This was interesting. I wondered what else Dr. Potter had been working on and why Gloria Scott hadn't taken it all when she had the chance.

I didn't ask my question out loud, but Gideon answered it anyway.

"Mother kept her notebooks in another, larger office down the hall. That's where she and Gloria did most of their everyday work. There is internet access in there, and faster computers. After the accident, when Gloria packed up her own stuff, she took some of Mother's notebooks with her. But the rest of Mother's final project is in here." He waved at the computer. "Gloria might be a good hacker, but there's no way to hack into this machine." Gideon tapped the keyboard to wake the computer up. The ball chair rolled a little as he sat down, but he steadied it with his legs. "The video of her illegally breaking and entering is right here," he said. "Watch."

We all gathered around the screen as a video file started playing. It clearly showed Gloria Scott entering the front door of house, glancing suspiciously over her shoulder every few seconds. That part faded black, then another camera caught her fleeing the house, past the big tree and through the iron gate. In the outdoor images, it was clear that a barking dog was chasing her, nipping at her heels. Her face was shadowed, but when she ran under a landscape light, I could see she was terrified.

"It doesn't look like Ms. Scott knows that dog," Charla remarked.

I agreed. "If this was Dr. Potter's pet, I don't think she'd be so freaked out."

"We just got the dog recently," Gideon told us. "Extra security."

"Is that the hard drive Ms. Scott wanted?" I asked, pointing at a small rectangular device on the table.

"Yes. Luckily, Kane scared her off," Gideon said. He grinned. "I named our new canine guardian myself. Kane is a Celtic name that means 'warrior.' I picked a dangerous name for a dangerous dog." He chuckled to himself.

I wondered where the dangerous fighter-dog Kane was now. I hoped he was far away from us.

Gideon handed a USB thumb drive to Mrs. Gray. "This is another copy of the security footage. I assume the case is going to be resolved quickly in court and that Ms. Scott will be turning over Mother's materials soon?"

"Yes," Mrs. Gray replied. "I believe this evidence will convince the judge that Gloria Scott intended to steal Dr. Potter's additional research. She'll be forced to give everything back to you and your sister. Given that she broke into your home, we may even be able to have her arrested."

"Good," Gideon said, shutting down the computer before walking with us back into the long hallway. "The sooner Leona and I can secure Mother's work, the better for everyone."

I thought about the newspaper headline we'd seen

online about Leona and Gideon wanting to honor their mother. I could see now that protecting her work was an important part of that. Dr. Potter was an important person, not just in Greenfield but across the country. Still, I wondered what they hoped to do with the work she left behind. Leona or Gideon didn't exactly come across as computer experts.

It seemed like Charla was thinking along similar lines. "What are you planning to do with Dr. Potter's final project?" she asked.

Gideon shrugged. "These things belonged to my mother," he said. "They should stay with our family."

It wasn't much of an answer, but it made sense. I know I would be protective if it were my family.

"There are rumors that Dr. Potter left a will," Mrs. Gray explained. "But no one can find it. Legally, since there are no instructions for what to do with her research, all Dr. Potter's work should go to her next of kin." That meant her children, Leona and Gideon.

Mrs. Gray turned to Gideon. "I'll ask if the judge will meet with us to review the new evidence and hopefully expedite the case."

Mrs. Gray placed the small USB drive safely in her purse. And with that, the meeting was over. It was time to go home.

We were headed toward the front door when I heard a creak behind me. I turned.

The door with the security lock clicked open, and Leona Potter stepped into the hall. She caught my eye and waved. Timidly, I waved back. She shut the door and stopped to check that the lock was secure before crossing the hall and entering the computer cave.

Charla grabbed my arm. "Come on, Jessie."

"Hmm." I pulled my gaze from the locked door and followed Charla out of the room. This was the house of a foremost expert on cybersecurity, but she had never felt the need for real-world security. After she died, Leona and Gideon had put the place on lockdown, with cameras, door codes, and even a dog.

It seemed to me that Dr. Potter had been a unique woman, but her children were downright strange.

Chapter 5

The Assistant's Assistant

At school on Tuesday, I was surprised to find that the video of Daniel as Hop-Man was still a hot topic. By now, I'd thought something else would have replaced the chants of "Hop away!" but apparently it was a slow news week at Greenfield Middle.

I caught up with Daniel before Mr. Masoud entered the art room.

"I know you're mad," I told him. "But sending the video around wasn't Charla's fault."

"I'm not mad," he said, staring at his shoelaces.

"I just don't want to talk about it."

"When you're ready, there's a mystery to solve," I told him. "Charla and I need our third musketeer." I hoped that might grab his attention, but Daniel kept his eyes glued to his shoes.

I went back to my seat. Today, we were doing something called pointillism. We had to draw a horse made entirely of dots. I was certain Daniel's horse would be fabulous, while mine would probably look like a blob with the measles.

At lunch, I shared my blobby measled art with Charla. Her painting was better than mine, but it still looked more like a connect-the-dots puzzle than a horse. We were both giggling about the results of our art attempts when Daniel passed by holding his tray.

He went to the back of the cafeteria like the day before, but this time Milo Miller sat with him, so he wasn't alone.

"He doesn't seem as upset anymore, does he?" Charla asked me.

I didn't want to stare, but I couldn't help turning around to look. "They're talking," I said. Daniel didn't really talk to anyone except me and Charla, so that was new. "It's hard to believe, but it seems like he's made a new friend."

Charla frowned. "I hope he's not replacing his old friends," she said.

"I wouldn't worry," I said. I couldn't imagine that Daniel wouldn't want to hang out with us ever again. That seemed impossible. I snuck another look to the back of the room.

Daniel was smiling! Laughing! That was good… and not good at the same time. Of course he should have other friends. But then again, I did really miss him. I sighed.

"Milo is such a sporty guy," Charla said. "What could he and Daniel even have in common?" She snuck a look at the two boys, who were now leaning over a magazine on the table. "Are they reading *Hop-Man*?" She was clearly starting to get jealous. A love of Hop-Man was a strong bond between her and Daniel. It was something that made their friendship special.

"It's hard to tell what they're reading from here," I said, though I was certain she'd recognize her favorite hero from this distance, even without her glasses. If Charla thought the boys were reading the new Hop-Man comic book, she was probably right.

She turned back to her sandwich and ate a few bites in silence. Then she changed the subject. "I'm still wondering how Gloria Scott managed to break into my mom's computer while we were using it."

I set aside my own worries about our friendship with Daniel for a moment. "Well, let's say there is something on Dr. Potter's hard drive that Ms. Scott wants," I began. "The papers she already took aren't enough, or there's something missing that she needs. There's no way to get into Dr. Potter's computer, so Ms. Scott goes to the house to grab the hard drive."

"She's not able to get it because the dog chases her out and the cameras record her escape," Charla said.

"She knows the video of her running across the grounds of Potter Manor makes her look suspicious, even if she didn't manage to get the hard drive," I said, making notes on my phone. "And she could go to jail for breaking in."

"So Ms. Scott wants to get rid of any evidence that

she was ever at the house," Charla said. "She hacks my mom's computer, deletes the email, and wipes the file from the laptop's hard drive."

"There seems to be a lot we still don't know," I said, wishing again that Daniel were there to help us. "What does Ms. Scott want that she doesn't already have?"

"And why would she think the only copy of a video was on my mom's computer?" Charla said thoughtfully. "This isn't 1982. There's never just one copy of anything."

I laughed. A few weeks ago, I'd told Charla about a mystery novel I'd read. It was about a stolen computer disk that held all of the operating secrets for some massive company. All I could think of while I read the book was how bizarre it was that there was only one disk and no backup files. The story took place in 1982, and Charla hadn't forgotten!

"What if…" Charla's eyes glimmered. "What if Mrs. Potter's assistant, Gloria, had a helper?"

"An assistant's assistant?" I chuckled. "Go on."

"My mom said there's proof that Ms. Scott was not near a computer when the computer got hacked, so maybe that means Ms. Scott had a helper. Someone else hacked into Mom's computer to erase the video while giving Ms. Scott an alibi."

"Interesting," I said. We hadn't met anyone yet who might be willing to help Gloria Scott, had we? Now that I thought about it, it seemed like most of the people involved with the case didn't like her very much.

"I think we need more details," Charla said. "Mom has all of the evidence and information she's collected so far at her office. We could go after school and see if there's anyone else we can investigate."

I had to talk to Ms. Surovsky after school to make up for skipping yesterday's newspaper meeting. "I can't—" I began when all of a sudden Ms. Surovsky appeared in the cafeteria doorway. Her eyes caught mine and she came straight over.

"I was looking for you, Jessie," she said. The black ringlets of her hair bounced when she talked. She wasn't just the faculty head of the *Greenfield Gabber*. She was my English teacher too. Ms. Surovsky pushed up her glasses and said, "I can't meet this afternoon. Do you have a minute to talk about your next feature now?"

Charla scooted over on the bench to make room between us. Ms. Surovsky sat down.

"Sure," I said. "As I mentioned in the note I wrote to you, I want to write about Dr. Clarisse Potter."

"The computer programmer who recently died?" Ms. Surovsky asked. When I nodded, she said, "It seems like everyone in town is talking about her lately. I think people would enjoy reading about her work, but is there something about the story that would make it relevant to the students here?"

It was the question I knew Ms. Surovsky would ask but wished she wouldn't. There was definitely something mysterious going on with Gloria Scott, but I knew that wasn't enough of a reason to write an article for the *Gabber*.

I had to be honest.

"I don't know yet," I said. "A quick search yesterday confirmed that Dr. Potter didn't go to school here, so I'm not sure what the connection is yet."

Charla had looked through her photos with the facial recognition software too. I'd kind of hoped she'd find a photo that could be my lead-in, but nothing had turned up. I still wasn't sure there would be a clear line between Dr. Potter and our school, but I wanted to keep exploring the subject.

Ms. Surovsky thought for a moment before giving her answer. "The deadline for the next issue is Monday. I know we don't have to put features in every issue, but I'd like to have another Jessie Alden piece. Your features so far have been great, and I have a feeling you'll find just the right angle for this one too. It will just take some time. What do you think? Can you make the deadline?"

"Monday is great," I said. "If I can't find a connection before then, I'll write about something else."

"Terrific." Ms. Surovsky stood up to go, but I stopped her. "Ever since we talked about what makes a good newspaper headline, I can't stop thinking about it. You had a word for when a headline doesn't match the story and is only there to get people to look. I've forgotten the word."

"Clickbait," Ms. Surovsky said. "A good headline should connect with readers, attract their attention, and most importantly, reflect what is in the article."

"And all that in ten words or less," I remembered.

"Clickbait uses headlines to get people on computers to click into an article. But it doesn't actually say anything useful." She gave a frustrated shrug. "When the newspapers get paid based on how many people follow a link, it raises the stakes. Headlines are often about views and money, rather than sharing accurate information."

I thought about the article Charla had shown me about Gideon and Leona Potter. The headline had read "Leona and Gideon Potter Strive to Honor Their Mother's Legacy."

Having met Leona and Gideon and asked them what they were planning to do with their mother's documents, it was clear to me that the headline wasn't just misleading. It was solidly wrong. It would have been better to say "Leona and Gideon Potter Begin Legal Battle for Their Mother's Work." That was eleven words. I challenged myself to come up with another way to say the same thing with one less word.

"Let me know how your research goes," Ms. Surovsky said, then she left the cafeteria.

"Lucky me. Looks like you're free this afternoon after all!" Charla grinned. "Meet me at the bike rack after school. We're going to find out if there really is an assistant's assistant."

Chapter 6

Close Encounter

Mrs. Gray was busy after school, so Charla and I had to wait awhile before going to her office. We did homework, had snacks, and then made funny videos of Pippen on Charla's phone. By the time Mrs. Gray finally drove us over to her office building, it was getting dark. Grandfather had given me permission to stay out if Charla's mom was okay with it, though.

"All public information about the case is in a file on my desk, next to my work computer. There's a lot in there. I'm not sure if any of it will be of help to you, but it's all okay for you to look at."

We passed by the security guard on the main floor, and Mrs. Gray continued, "My personal laptop is on the couch. Mind plugging it in again for me?"

"Are you sure?" Charla raised an eyebrow. "That didn't go so well last time."

Her mom probably thought she was talking about the erased evidence, but I knew Charla meant Daniel and his video.

"Just don't get hacked, okay?" Mrs. Gray said as if that were a choice.

"Sure thing, Mom," Charla replied, rolling her eyes.

Her mom left us by the elevator bay and told the security guard she'd be back in an hour to pick us up. He said he'd check on us after a while.

Charla and I went to the seventh floor.

Mrs. Gray's office had incredible views of Greenfield, looking out over the river. I could see twinkling lights inside the apartments along the boardwalk. It was so beautiful that I would have liked to sit by the oversized window all night, but we didn't have much time before Charla's mom came back. Charla dragged me away from the view.

She had the laptop open. "I want to start with emails," she explained. "Maybe Mom fell for a phishing scam that gave someone access to her computer."

"Fishing?" I asked. "I do like trout." I was kidding. I knew she was talking about some kind of computer hacking thing, but I didn't know exactly how it worked.

"Letter *P* and letter *H*," Charla said. "Phishing." She explained it to me. "Phishing is when a hacker tries tricking someone into giving up personal information. Then they use what they've learned to log in to the person's accounts." She scrolled through her mom's emails. "The subject lines of phishing emails look like they come from a trustworthy sender, like your bank or favorite store. Once you open the email, it might ask you to click a link or send a response containing your log-in info or other personal information."

"And after that, they have access to your computer?" I asked.

"Depending on the information they are able to get out of you, sure," Charla said. She studied the screen. "I don't see anything fishy."

"Is that letters *P* and *H* or letter *F*?" I asked, and we both laughed.

Then I thought of something serious. "Charla," I began, "the hacker wasn't just snooping around your mom's email. They seemed to have access to the entire computer." I reminded her how the cursor jumped around before the screen went black.

"Good point. Change of plans." Charla rubbed her eyes and looked at the computer again. "I think phishing might be the wrong approach," she said. "The hacker might have gained remote access."

I knew what that meant. Once, when my own computer was acting up, I called Charla for help but she couldn't come over. I agreed to give her remote access, and she was able to take over my cursor from her own computer. Charla fixed the problem, and my computer hasn't been glitchy since.

"My mom uses remote access sometimes to get stuff off her work computer while she's on her laptop at home," Charla said. "I connected the two work-spaces and taught her how to switch smoothly back and forth."

"Could someone have set up a connection without your mom knowing?" I asked.

Charla looked unsure. "I don't think so. Then again, I'm not an amazing hacker. I *fix* people's computer problems."

"Well, you're good at that," I told Charla. "You could start a business. I mean, you're already helping so many people. You should get to make some money!" I immediately regretted giving her the idea. "But you can't charge me for help, okay? Friend discount."

"I can't charge my mom either," Charla said. "She'd be my biggest customer."

"It's hard to start a computer business when you work for friends and family," I mused.

"When you start charging people to solve their mysteries, I'll start charging to fix their computers," Charla said. We both knew that meant we'd never get paid. We did what we did because we liked it, not for cash.

Mrs. Gray's files for the Potter case were sitting on the desk, right where she said they'd be. It was a thick collection of notes and evidence.

"There's one big thing I don't get," I said as we spread papers from the file neatly across the desk. "If the hacker knew about the security footage, why not try to delete it from the Potters' computer as well?" The question nagged at me. "Removing the file from your mom's computer is just a temporary setback."

"I've been thinking about that too," Charla said. "All I can come up with is that because Dr. Potter's hard drive was in a room without internet, perhaps the hacker thought that there were only two copies: one on my mom's computer and another on Dr. Potter's computer."

"That would explain it," I replied. "If she could get rid of both, that would be the end of the security footage." I still thought the hacker would assume there were other video copies, but this made sense—for now.

Every time we said "hacker," all I could think was Gloria Scott. It was hard not to think of her as the one and only suspect in this case. I tried to open my mind to all the facts in front of us. I didn't want to prejudge the evidence. I just wanted to see what popped off the file pages and seemed important.

"Wow," I said after reading a few articles about Dr. Potter. "She was a huge deal in the programming world!"

I found a photo of her that we hadn't seen before. The picture was taken when she was right out of college. She was wearing black pants with a white blouse and pearl necklace. I showed Charla.

"Ha! She used to dress like my mom!" Charla exclaimed. "Do you think someday my mom might dye her hair like a rainbow and get a tattoo?" She gushed, "That would be awesome."

It was hard to imagine Mrs. Gray with a tattoo, but looking at this photo, it was hard to imagine young Dr. Potter with one too.

I found a copy of her obituary in the file. It had a lot of information about her life, like where she went to school and her employment history.

"She worked for a couple of really big tech companies," I reported. "And NASA! Maybe she helped with a rocket ship," I said, but Charla wasn't listening. She was doing her own research.

There was a line in the obituary that stuck out at me. "Hey, Charla," I said, getting her attention. "Listen to this: 'Dr. Potter is survived by her two sons and daughter.'" I set down the obituary. "We know about Leona and Gideon. Did your mom mention a third sibling?"

"Three?" Charla looked confused. "No, Mom is only representing Gideon and Leona in the lawsuit. That's strange. Wouldn't all three be working together to get their mother's work back from Gloria Scott?"

I shrugged. "I don't know who—"

Suddenly the elevator dinged outside of the office, and I heard someone step off. We weren't expecting Charla's mom to be back for a while, and the footsteps did not sound like the click of Mrs. Gray's high heels. These shoes squeaked against the tile floor, meaning they had rubber soles.

Thinking we would be alone in the office, we hadn't bothered to close the door. I wondered if I should rush forward, close it, and lock it.

Charla took one look at my nervous expression and said, "It's just the security guard, Jessie. He told my mom he'd come check on us."

"Oh, right," I said, feeling calmer. But my heart began to race again when a voice called out, "Is someone here?"

It was a deep, gravelly voice, and its owner sounded genuinely surprised that someone else was in the building.

"That's not the security guard," I whispered to Charla. "He would have known we were here."

I grabbed the closest thing I could find to defend myself: a crystal paperweight. Charla picked up a stapler. We were ready to knock down the intruder and make a run for the stairs when the man stepped into view.

The man with the rubber-soled shoes blocked the entire doorway. He was big—not just tall, but large everywhere. I wasn't sure what he wanted, but I didn't want to hang around to find out.

"I'm surprised anyone is here so late," he remarked, staring at us with cold, dark eyes.

"Me too," I whispered to Charla. I didn't feel comfortable that someone else was here when the office should have been closed. What if he was here to steal the file we were looking at? Could this be the hacker's assistant?

My heart was racing. I took a deep breath and steadied myself, preparing to conk the man in the head with my paperweight if I had to.

Charla, however, set down the stapler and began cleaning up the papers across the desk and putting them back into the files. "My mom is picking us up soon," she said without any emotion. Just the facts.

"Okay, no problem," the man said as he stepped back out of the doorway.

"Where'd he go?" I whispered to Charla, my voice tense. I wanted her to stop cleaning up and prepare to run.

Charla whispered to me, "Jessie, I think your powers of observation start to disappear when you're worried."

I didn't understand.

"It's the night shift. He's here to clean up," she said.

A moment later, the man returned with a can of wood polish and a dusting cloth. Once he was standing in full light, I could see he was wearing a gray shirt and pants. He had an ID badge for the building, and in bold black letters it said "CUSTODIAN."

It was just the janitor! Of course there'd be someone cleaning the office at night when the lawyers were away. I took a calming breath and set down the paperweight. I was embarrassed that I'd missed the clues.

Charla put her hand on my shoulder. "You can't be the best detective in Greenfield *all* the time," she said with a laugh.

"Good thing I have you on my team," I told her while I helped put the last items back in the case file.

We left the office and went back down the elevator.

I said, "If Daniel had been here, he'd have had some superspy gear and would have known the janitor was coming long before the guy showed up."

"He does like spy gear," Charla remarked. "I think we've let him stew long enough. Let's try to talk to him tomorrow."

I agreed. I was excited at the thought of Daniel being with us the next time we were out looking for clues.

After a while, Mrs. Gray arrived to pick us up. As we climbed into her car, she asked, "How'd it go?"

"We didn't figure out who the hacker is," I said. "Not yet."

There was a quiet pause, then Charla said, "Mom, based on what we discovered, I have a very important question."

"Sure," Mrs. Gray said. "What is it?"

Charla looked at me and winked, then asked her mom, "If you got a tattoo, what would you get?"

Her mom didn't hesitate. "A big heart on my forehead that says, 'I love Charla.'"

"That's what I thought," Charla said, laughing.

"I'd get the same one," I said, pointing to the space between my eyes. "Right here."

Later that night, I went to sleep thinking about Dr. Potter. She'd gone from that young girl in neat sweaters to a cutting-edge rebel. She'd worked her way through many companies to become an important programmer. Her story was inspiring and worth telling. I just needed a connection between her and my school. There had to be something I'd missed. But what could it be?

Chapter 7

Listening In

The next morning, Charla came to school wearing a new shirt she'd made herself. It said "Gone Phishing." Instead of a fishing rod, it had a computer keyboard as the graphic.

We met on the steps outside the school. We always came to school early because Charla and I both liked to have extra time to get organized for the day. "Hey, I understand what that shirt means now," I said. "The jokes are funnier when I actually get them."

Charla smiled proudly. "Some of the kids in coding

club have asked if I'd sell my shirts, but I'm still too mad at whoever sent out Daniel's video." Charla shrugged. "Maybe I'll think about it once this whole thing passes."

"Why can't you track whoever sent the video around?" Although I wished I understood more about computer technology, I was glad Charla knew so much. My head was full of school projects, upcoming tests, and the stress of not having an article topic for the newspaper. If someone told me to add even just a few coding skills to my crowded brain, I might explode.

"The video was forwarded by a lot of people," Charla said. "I might be able to figure it out with enough time, but it wouldn't be easy. For now, it's much simpler to be mad at the entire coding club." She shrugged. "I'll get over feeling mad, but not until Daniel gets over it too."

As we walked inside and headed to our lockers, we ran into a new problem.

"Oh no," I said. Usually, there were flyers posted on the school walls about sporting events or student government, but today the walls featured giant, poster-sized photos.

"I don't think he's getting over anything once he sees this," I said, feeling a knot grow in my stomach.

The photos, snapped from screen captures and blown up extra large, were of Daniel in his Hop-Man makeup, rolling around the floor of his room. There were probably about ten posters in the hallway, and who knows how many were tacked up other places around school. This was bad. Really, really bad.

"Should we tear them down?" I asked Charla, who was staring at one of the pictures with her jaw wide-open.

She responded by grabbing the nearest photo, ripping it off the wall, and turning it into little bitty confetti. "Good thing we got here early."

Suddenly Charla's eyes opened wide, and she stopped ripping up the photo. "Press the pause key, Jessie! Whoever made these must be here early too. The pictures had to have been posted this morning." She turned to me. "Let's sleuth out who is taping these up. If it's someone from coding club…" There was fire in her eyes. She was furious at the idea that someone from her favorite club might have taken Daniel's video and taken an additional step to embarrass him.

"It's okay," a voice said from behind us. We both turned to see Daniel. I was surprised to see him at school early and even more surprised that he was talking to us.

"Don't worry about the posters," he said. "I think solving one mystery at a time is good enough."

"But…" Charla tore down a second poster and made more confetti with it. "I was mad before and now I'm madder."

"Furious?" I suggested. "Fuming? Annoyed? Outraged?"

"All of those," Charla said. "And more." She snatched a third poster.

Daniel took it from her and ripped it up himself. "I don't want to be upset anymore," he said. "I'm done being angry. And embarrassed. I'm moving on." He put the torn poster in the trash can. "You know what would help?" he asked with a small smile.

"Solving the mystery around a famous programmer and her mysterious assistant?" I asked.

When Daniel nodded, I smiled so wide I could feel my face stretching. "Glad to have the third musketeer back."

"All for one," Daniel said.

"And one for all," Charla finished.

Daniel was excited to get up-to-date on everything we'd discovered. Curiously, he seemed to know a lot about the case already. On the way to class, Milo tossed an air high-five to Daniel, who fired back with his own air slap.

"New friend?" Charla asked.

"I guess," Daniel said tentatively. "He's in my English class and asked to hang out. We played video games together over the weekend." He pushed back his hair. "The game was fun, but all he wanted to talk about was Charla's mom's case." Daniel tipped his head toward me. "He read your last *Gabber* article, Jessie. The one about us working together to solve a mystery. He assumed I'd know all the details of this mystery too."

That explained why Daniel already knew about the case. He'd been talking about it with Milo. We had a few minutes before Mr. Masoud came in, so we stopped in our usual spot in the middle of the class.

I asked Daniel, "Did Milo say anything that seemed like a clue? I mean, he mows the grass at the manor, so he's there all the time."

"Nope." Daniel shook his head. "I think that's why he's interested," he said. "He has been working there since before Dr. Potter died. He knows Gloria Scott and likes her. Milo doesn't understand how she got mixed up in all this drama."

"Did he say anything else about Ms. Scott?" Charla asked. "Like if she's got an assistant?"

"Nothing else," Daniel said. It was time for class to start. "Just that she's really nice and smart, and he'd hate to see her get in trouble."

This was *not* what I was expecting someone who knew Gloria Scott to say about her. I wanted to ask more, but Mr. Masoud took his place at the front of the room. "Class, take your seats," he announced.

Charla said quickly, "On Saturday, there's going to be a court hearing for the lawsuit. Mom will be arguing that Gloria Scott should be arrested, since they have the proof of her breaking and entering."

"Arrested?" Daniel said, as Mr. Masoud gave us all a severe look that meant we'd better take our seats ASAP. "I'd better tell Milo. He's not going to like this news."

Charla continued, "We should go to the hearing and see what happens. If we're lucky, maybe we'll get a chance to talk to Gloria Scott ourselves."

"Daniel Garza. Charla Gray. Jessie Alden," Mr. Masoud called. "You have three seconds to get to your desks or else."

We didn't know what "or else" meant, and we didn't want to find out. Two seconds later, we were in our seats and class began.

∘ ∘ ∘

Usually, Saturdays were Just Jessie time in the boxcar that sat behind my house. The boxcar was mine and my siblings' clubhouse, and Just Jessie time was my time to study, write, think, or just hang out with friends.

All week, I'd been looking forward to my Just Jessie time, but going to the courthouse for Ms. Scott's hearing was more important.

Charla, Daniel, and I rode to the courthouse with Mrs. Gray. When we arrived, the media was gathered on the street in front of the building. Reporters shouted at Charla's mom, asking for a statement. I was thinking about the headline I would write if I were reporting about the case.

Ten words or less. Interesting hook. Truthful. Not clickbait.

Clarisse Potter's Assistant
Accused of Stealing from Estate

That wasn't bad and was only eight words. Personally, I'd be intrigued enough to read that article.

We moved past the clamoring journalists with their TV crews and went inside the courthouse. Unlike the sidewalk outside, it was very quiet. Mrs. Gray had successfully avoided making a statement, though Leona and Gideon had stopped to say they hoped the judge would send Gloria Scott to jail as soon as possible.

Charla, Daniel, and I had dressed up. I was wearing a floral dress and a sweater. Daniel was wearing a suit and tie. Charla was in a skirt and blouse. It was almost a little strange seeing her wear something without a computer joke printed on it. We looked nice, but we still weren't allowed past the building's foyer.

"Stay here." Mrs. Gray showed us to a bench outside

the judge's chambers. She went into the office, and Leona and Gideon followed.

"Look." Charla pointed at a young woman who had just walked into the building. From the way people were looking at her, I could tell it was Gloria Scott. She and her lawyer disappeared behind the same heavy wooden door Charla's mom and the Potters had entered.

It wasn't long before Charla's mom returned. She was frowning, and she gave us a small shake of her head.

"No?" Charla asked.

"No," Mrs. Gray confirmed.

We all went outside, where Gloria Scott's attorney was speaking to the press. The journalists were gathered tightly around her. They didn't notice us watching.

"Today is a good day for justice," the lawyer said, clutching her briefcase. The lawyer was alone. Ms. Scott was nowhere to be seen. "The judge said there's not enough evidence for a breaking and entering charge. It is entirely possible that Ms. Scott was invited to the house, which was also her former place of employment." She leaned into the microphones and said clearly, "Ms. Scott is free to go home."

Just then, one of the reporters noticed Charla's mom. "Mrs. Gray! Mrs. Gray!" He led a rush across the courthouse steps to get a comment from her.

"How are Leona and Gideon taking the news?" a reporter shouted.

"I—" Mrs. Gray began as Gideon and Leona came out of the courthouse.

"We are obviously upset," Leona interrupted. "Today was *not* a good day for justice."

"More evidence will come out," Mrs. Gray told the press. "This case is not over. I have full confidence that Ms. Scott will be required to return Dr. Potter's research in due course and that she will be held accountable for breaking in to try to steal what is not hers."

With that, the press moved on, anxious to file their stories. I hoped that what happened here today would be accurately represented and made a mental note to review the local news websites later in the afternoon.

Once it was quiet again, I asked Leona if I could interview her about Dr. Potter. "I'd like to learn more about your mom," I told her. "I'm looking for an angle that will let me write about her for our school paper."

"Mom would have loved that," Leona said, brightening. "She enjoyed helping and mentoring students." Gideon pulled up in his car and honked the horn. "Come by the manor tomorrow," Leona told me as she opened the passenger-side door to get in.

I was thrilled. My final deadline was Monday. If I could get the information I needed tomorrow, that would give me the night to write up something for Ms. Surovsky. Fingers crossed that I'd find the connection I was looking for.

As the Potters drove off, Mrs. Gray mentioned she had one last thing to do before we could leave. She asked us to wait outside and walked up the stairs, back to the courthouse.

Daniel had been pretty much silent all day. He'd hardly said a word since we'd arrived at the courthouse. I wasn't surprised, since he often got quiet when he was around a lot of people. I also wasn't surprised that he started talking a mile a minute once everyone was gone. We'd caught him up as best we could, but he still had a lot of questions.

"How could Gloria Scott have hacked your mom's

computer, Charla?" He didn't wait for us to answer. He asked another. "What was Ms. Scott's alibi? Where was she when your computer got hacked?"

He barely paused for breath between the rapid-fire questions.

"Why did Gloria need the hard drive?" I thought we could answer that one, but he barreled on. "She was Dr. Potter's assistant, so I bet she used to have a key to the house. Does she still? We should find out."

I pulled out my phone and started taking notes on everything Daniel was saying. If only Daniel had been there all along to ask these questions at the right times.

"Oh yeah," Daniel continued. "And what was Dr. Potter even working on that everyone wants it so badly?" That was an excellent question as well.

Just then, the side door to the courthouse opened and Gloria Scott walked out into the sunshine with her lawyer. She looked much younger than Leona and Gideon, and she was wearing a black dress with a wide silver belt. Fashionable but not flashy. Her dark hair was twisted into a bun at the back of her neck and tied with a colorful purple scarf.

"There she is," said Charla, a hint of admiration in her voice. "I wish we could hear what she was saying."

Even from a distance, we could tell that Ms. Scott and her lawyer were arguing.

"Charla, your wish is my command," Daniel said with a dramatic bow. After doing a little genie dance, he announced, "Ta-da!" and pulled a small black box out of his jacket pocket. He tugged on a silver antenna and it grew until it was about the length of a fishing pole.

"What is *that?*" I asked.

"A listening device of course," he said. "Duh." He chuckled.

"Of course," I muttered. I should have known that Daniel would have some kind of spy trick up his sleeve. Wherever he got his supplies, he was likely their best customer.

Charla was excited about the technology. "How does it work?"

"This box connects to an app on my phone," Daniel explained.

Charla begged to see the app. "It can record conversations?" she asked.

Daniel nodded.

Charla glanced from where we were to where Ms. Scott and her lawyer were standing. "Can it pick up sounds that far away?"

"Farther," Daniel said, grinning widely. "Much farther." He pointed the antenna at Ms. Scott and pressed a button on his phone. Then he put in his earbuds.

"You'll tell us what they say?" said Charla. "In real time?"

"Hang on." I needed to think about what we were doing. "I'm a little uncomfortable with eavesdropping."

"They're in public," Daniel replied. "If they wanted privacy, they could have stayed inside."

"I suppose it's okay," I agreed. If they were talking about something really private, they would have found a more secure place to do it.

"What are they saying, Daniel?" Charla asked. She rolled her hand to tell him to hurry up.

"'This won't end until Gideon and Leona get what they deserve,'" Daniel said in a serious voice. It took me a moment to realize that he was imitating Gloria, who was standing with her hands on her hips.

"'What are you planning, Gloria?'" With that, Daniel crossed his arms to show that the lawyer was speaking.

Hands back on hips, Daniel gave us Gloria's reply: "I need to get to the safe!" To cap off his performance, Daniel pretended to be putting something in a combination safe and twisting the lock to secure it.

"Safe?" Charla asked Daniel. This was new information.

"That's what she said," Daniel confirmed.

"Then we need to find that safe," Charla said.

I nodded. "And figure out what's inside."

Chapter 8

Vanishing Act

On Sunday morning I rode my bike to Potter Manor by myself. I had to find a way to link Dr. Potter to Greenfield Middle School so I could write my article. It was due the next day, and I still had a lot of work to do. And yet there was much more on my mind than putting together an article for Ms. Surovsky. Daniel had given us a great list of questions, and I thought that as long as I was interviewing Leona Potter for the newspaper, I might also be able to get a few answers for our mystery.

Daniel and Charla had asked to come along, but I felt like I could get more information, snoop better, and maybe even get an amazing scoop for the *Gabber* if I was on my own.

The gate was open, so I rode up to the manor and parked my bike by a big tree. Like before, Milo was working on the lawn. He looked super focused and he had his earbuds in, so I didn't interrupt him.

I knocked on the door of the big old house, and Leona answered. She seemed overdressed for a meeting with a twelve-year-old. Flowered dress. Heels. Hair swept up into a twist. Maybe she thought I'd be taking pictures for the paper?

"Jessie," she greeted me. "Nice of you to come." When she stepped aside, I was stunned to find Kane, the supposedly vicious fighting dog, sitting patiently at her side.

"Good boy, Kane." Leona gave the black Labrador a pat on the head. In the evidence video, it was impossible to see what kind of dog had chased Gloria Scott off the Potter property, but up close, Kane was clearly a Lab. Labs are not known to be guard dogs. They're generally gentle and friendly.

I took a chance and slowly reached my hand toward the dog. Kane sniffed my fingers and wagged his tail. "Can I pet him?" I asked. Grandfather had taught me to always ask before petting a strange dog.

"Of course," Leona said. "He's a sweetie." I realized she hadn't been in the room when Gideon had told us Kane was a bloodthirsty killer.

As Kane licked my hand, I asked Leona. "Any other dogs around here?"

"One is enough," she said. "I've been training him myself." She firmly instructed Kane to heel, and he followed us into the parlor with the two couches.

We sat exactly as we had before, with me on the red couch and her on the yellow one.

"Okay, shoot," Leona said, then laughed. "I mean you can ask me anything."

"Thanks." I opened the note on my phone where I'd typed out Daniel's questions and added a few of my own.

"Do you know where Ms. Scott was last Sunday night?" That was when Charla's mom's computer got hacked and Daniel's video was sent out.

Ms. Potter tilted her head at me and squinted as if the question was unexpected. Still, she answered. "Ms. Scott claims she was at a restaurant with her father," Leona scoffed. "She even has the receipt from the meal." I could tell she wasn't buying the alibi. "If Ms. Scott is half as good a hacker as my mother claimed, she could have stolen that video from her phone or a small laptop logged in to the restaurant's Wi-Fi." She shook her head. "Liars lie. That's what they do."

I typed in her answer and then moved on to the next question.

"Does Ms. Scott have a key to the house?"

Leona tilted her head again, then asked, "Are you sure you're doing an article about my mother?" She gave me a sideways look. "These questions sound a lot like the ones the police asked when I first reported Ms. Scott's theft."

"Oh." I cleared my throat. "I'm just trying to find an angle into my article," I said. "I thought I'd open with the court case, then go back to Dr. Potter's programming career."

"I see," Leona said, seeming to accept my explanation.

She didn't answer about the house key though. "Next question?"

"What exactly was your mom working on when she died? It must have been something amazing."

"Ah." Leona became animated as she launched into the explanation. "These days, regular antivirus software is not enough to stop major cyberattacks." She asked if I'd read the recent news stories about companies not only getting their data hacked but being forced to pay ransom to the villains who'd hijacked their information. She mentioned a large hospital chain and an oil company that both had to sacrifice services while they paid off the hackers.

I'd heard about both stories. A cyberattack had also happened in Greenfield last summer, and the supermarket had been forced to close when all the cash registers were knocked offline for a day.

Leona shared: "Mother was passionate about protecting people's personal information. When she died, she was right in the middle of a big breakthrough on an open-source program that would help companies secure their data better than ever before."

This part was a bit more advanced for me. I typed out Leona's exact words and put a star by them so I wouldn't forget to ask Charla what some of the tech terms meant.

"My mother, as you know, was a genius," Leona continued. "This project could change the world. Gideon and I will finish what she started. We need all her notes and the information on her hard drive to piece it together."

"Can you write code?" I asked, wondering who would actually finish Dr. Potter's work.

"No, but Gideon and I have a plan. Just because we aren't programmers, it doesn't mean we can't oversee the project."

So this is what they'd meant by securing Dr. Potter's legacy. I'd thought it was about donating her papers to a university or a museum, but it was actually about getting her work out there for the world to use. Knowing that Dr. Potter wanted people and companies to be protected from hackers, it made perfect sense. Her program was her legacy too.

I focused my next questions on the basic facts of Dr.

Potter's life, hoping I'd find the link for my article. Where did she grow up? Where did she go to college? Where was her first job? Nothing connected. When Dr. Potter moved to Greenfield, it was because she wanted to live in a quiet town where she could focus on her work.

I had one more pressing question on my list. It was the one I was most nervous to ask. "I read that Dr. Potter had three children. I've only met you and Gideon," I said. "What can you tell me about your brother or sister?"

I don't know if Leona was planning to answer or not, because the instant I finished asking the question, all the lights in the manor went out. It was daytime and there was still plenty of light streaming in from the windows, but the sudden quiet was concerning. All the little hums and beeps a house normally makes fell into a deep stillness.

"What's going on?" said Leona, jumping to her feet. Kane started howling—not yips or barks but full-on crying.

"Jessie, hurry!" Leona said dramatically. She dashed from the room and I followed. Even in my sneakers, I had trouble keeping up with her clicking high heels.

I was still a few steps behind her as she burst into the computer room.

"The hard drive!" Leona screamed. She pointed to the table where the drive had been sitting the last time I was in the house. "It's gone!"

She rushed back out of the room and sprinted to the end of the hallway. There was a doorway to the right of the security camera. I hadn't noticed it the first time I visited, but I did see that the green light on the camera was off. It wasn't recording right now.

The side door was cracked open. It led outside, into the yard. When Leona opened the door all the way, I saw Kane running across the grass at top speed. He was barking loudly as he ran toward the front gate, but even now, this was not a scary dog. His chest bounced in a goofy, puppylike way when he ran. Now that I knew him, I could see that Kane was a lot more of a "play with me" dog than a "get off my lawn" killer.

The main gate was closed. Whoever Kane was chasing had gotten away.

"I can't believe it!" Leona was furious. "Gloria Scott stole the hard drive!"

I didn't understand how Leona knew it was Ms. Scott that had broken into the house, but she seemed certain.

"Obviously, she opened the front door while we were in the parlor," Leona told me. "She scurried down the hallway, exactly like last time. You saw it on the security footage." I let myself imagine Gloria Scott in the hallway. "This time, Gloria managed to get the drive and escape out the back door!"

I'd seen the dog running toward the gate. And still, I had no idea how Ms. Potter knew for certain that it was Ms. Scott who had broken in today.

"Sorry, Jessie," Ms. Potter told me. "No more questions today. I need to find Gideon and tell him what happened."

"Sure," I said. "Thanks for—" *Wait a minute*, I thought. "Did you say there was security camera footage of Ms. Potter in the hallway the night she originally broke in?" I had *imagined* Gloria Scott in the hallway, but in the actual video footage, I'd only seen her entering the house and later being chased by the dog. If the hallway camera had captured her entering the computer room, it wasn't in the video evidence that Gideon had shown Mrs. Gray when we visited.

Leona was distracted. She was staring at her phone while Kane continued barking loudly at the front gate. The electricity was still off. "Really, Jessie. No more interview questions." It was kind of her to add "I'd be happy to have you come back another time."

"I understand," I said, letting my question drop. "Thanks for meeting me today."

Ms. Potter gave me a slight nod, then went back inside the side door. I started across the lawn to pick up my bike.

Milo was no longer around. The lawn looked freshly mowed, with long cut lines across the grass. He'd probably finished up and gone home already, which meant that he'd narrowly missed seeing whoever had stolen the hard drive.

It was either very brave or very foolish to rob a house in the middle of the day, but it had worked. I needed to call Charla and Daniel right away to tell them what happened: someone had taken the hard drive, and the prime suspect was Gloria Scott.

Chapter 9

Person of Interest

On Monday, I was waiting in the hallway when Charla and Daniel hurried toward me. I had texted last night to fill them in, but I wanted to go over the details again in person.

"It's hard to believe that Gloria Scott robbed Potter Manor in the middle of the day," I said, jumping right in without even saying hi. "I've gone over the whole morning a million times in my head. It's stuck on repeat!"

Charla put her hand on my shoulder and looked me

straight in the eyes. "You need to calm down," she said. "Solving the mystery is important, but you're obsessing." Today her shirt said "Programmed for Success." The letters were printed in red glitter puffy paint. It was one of her best designs yet.

"Let's talk about Daniel instead," Charla continued. "That should throw Jessie's brain in a new direction." We both turned to face Daniel.

"Uh, no thanks." Daniel blushed. "Let's not talk about Daniel. Ever."

"The posters are gone," Charla said, looking for another topic. "The school seems to have moved on to talking about the football team."

"What does Milo think about the team's chances this year?" I asked Daniel. "JJ mentioned that he interviewed a bunch of the players for the *Gabber*, but he didn't get a quote from Milo. Is he excited to start the season?" Practices were in full swing, and the team's first game was coming up in a few weeks.

Daniel shrugged. "I didn't ask him." Then he said, "When I'm hanging out with Milo, he doesn't usually want to talk about sports."

"Maybe we could all go to a game sometime," I suggested.

"I'd go," Charla said. "But only to cheer for Milo."

"Sure. I'll ask him about it in class," Daniel replied, even though I was pretty certain he didn't have any interest in football. Sports just weren't his thing.

"Speaking of after-school stuff," I said, "are you still going to try out for the play?" Daniel would be such an amazing actor. I really hoped he wasn't giving up. The newspaper had done an article about the auditions, which were coming up soon.

"I'm not interested anymore," he said firmly. "The whole video mess made me realize that I don't like being in public. When I draw or paint, I don't have to worry about what anyone else thinks."

"You'd be amazing in the school play though," I said.

"I can't," Daniel told us. I'd already gotten my books from my locker, and Charla was all set for the morning. We walked together to Daniel's locker. He said, "I just can't have people looking at me like that. It makes me too nervous."

"As a Hop-Man expert," Charla began. "I thought

your video was hop-a-rific." She gave a Hop-Man jump and landed a foot away, then turned back. "Anyone who knows the comic would tell you that your face paint was perfect and your acting was worthy of an award."

"An a-*wart!*" I laughed at my own pun.

Charla giggled, but Daniel didn't smile. He got his books and closed his locker door.

"The video was really great," Charla told him. "Non-Hoppers just didn't get it. That's the only reason people were so mean."

"If I say I'll consider going to audition, will you stop bothering me about it?" Daniel asked Charla.

The bell rang. It was time for class.

"What do you want me to bother you about instead?" Charla asked. "What could possibly be as interesting as your future acting career?"

Daniel rolled his eyes. "I'll come up with something." Then he turned to me. "Moving on. Let's talk about Jessie now."

"That topic is O-V-E-R," I spelled. "I told you what happened yesterday. We're all caught up."

I didn't think there was more to talk about until Daniel asked, "Did you find an angle for your next feature?"

"Oh, right. That." I was in big trouble, and I knew it. "I should have found another topic, but my brain was too full of what happened at the Potter place. I messed up, and I don't know what to do."

I had ended up not sending Ms. Surovsky anything. Mostly, I was scared of what Ms. Surovsky was going to say. I thought she might tell me I couldn't be a journalist for the school paper anymore. All my ideas about going green, not to mention my future articles, would poof away. It would be devastating.

We went into our classroom. Mr. Masoud had on a brown beret today and was waving his paintbrush like a magic wand. "To your seats," he commanded as if he were casting some kind of spell that would drag us into our chairs.

"I'll have to explain to Ms. Surovsky later," I said. "It's not going to be a fun conversation."

"I'm sure she'll understand," Charla said, trying to cheer me up.

"Maybe you can skip this week," Daniel put in. "Write something even better next time?"

"I don't know," I said, wishing I had at least come up with some other idea. Anything else.

Mr. Masoud pointed his paintbrush wand at me and said, "Jessie Alden, clear your mind and let the art flow." For a split second I wondered if he could have known about what happened at Potter Manor or my newspaper troubles. But that was impossible. More likely, all of that stress was showing up on my face.

Still, Mr. Masoud's pretend magic spell helped break the loop in my head. When I began to paint, I was able to forget about the missing hard drive and my unfinished newspaper article—at least for a little bit.

I'd never gotten so into an art project before. As I put the finishing touches on my painting, I was surprised to see that it had turned out pretty well. Even Mr. Masoud was impressed. He studied my landscape and then looked at the paintbrush he'd used as a magic wand.

"I think this thing might actually have powers," he said with a chuckle. "This is the best artwork you've created so far, Jessie. The perspective is measured, and the focal point looks like an actual mountain!"

"Definitely not a blob," Daniel said, coming over to see what I'd done.

"And no measles," Charla added.

The bell rang. Art class was over.

"Can I use your project as an example for the next class?" Mr. Masoud asked. "I'd like to show the other students what can happen when you really let your creativity flow."

I hesitated. There was a part of me that felt like Daniel when the Hop-Man video was being passed around. I didn't want other students judging my work. Then again, it was the best I'd done, and though I wasn't usually much of an artist, I was proud of my landscape.

"Sure," I said. "You can keep—"

"We gotta go!" Charla grabbed my arm in one hand and Daniel's backpack strap in her other. "Sorry, Mr. Masoud," she said in a rush. "Keep the art. I need Jessie."

Mr. Masoud looked hard at the three of us. "Another mystery?" he asked.

"A big development," Charla said, holding up her cell phone. She quickly added, "I promise my phone was off until the bell rang."

"Go on, then," Mr. Masoud told us. "I can't stand in the way of a big development." He took my painting to his desk. Before we left the room, he said to me, "I look forward to seeing your next article in the *Gabber*."

I sighed. I didn't want to admit I'd hit a dead end and Ms. Surovsky might never let me write anything else. "We'll see" was all I could manage in response.

◦ ◦ ◦

As excited as Charla was about her big development, she didn't get a chance to share it with me and Daniel until later in the day. We kept moving from class to class. I passed Charla in the hall a few times but never stopped long enough to find out what she'd discovered. Between bells two and three, I saw Daniel by the drinking fountain and asked if he'd talked to Charla yet. "Nope!" he shouted before rushing off to his next class.

I was running to the cafeteria to see my friends and

find out the big news when Ms. Surovsky stopped me in the hallway.

"Jessie!"

My stomach sank. English class wasn't until fifth bell, and I'd been ducking around corners all morning avoiding her.

"I've been expecting your article," she said. I could hear the disappointment in her voice.

I looked toward the cafeteria and saw Charla and Daniel go in together. I blew out a heavy breath. The mystery was important, but so was the *Gabber*. I turned my whole body toward Ms. Surovsky so I wouldn't be distracted.

"I'm sorry," I told my teacher. "I can't find any connection between Dr. Potter and the school."

Ms. Surovsky was wearing her reading glasses and tipped them down to look at me over the frames. "Were you able to come up with a backup subject?"

"I—" I was so upset at myself. I should have used yesterday afternoon to find something else to write about, but after everything that happened at the manor, I just didn't feel like it. No excuses.

My teacher looked as disappointed as I had feared she would be. "You know how the newspaper works, Jessie. I gave you extra time. You had until today."

I struggled to stay focused on Ms. Surovsky, but I couldn't stop thinking about the Potters and the stolen hard drive.

Ms. Surovsky was talking about editing and layouts and printing issues at the copy machine. I vaguely heard her going over what I already knew: the newspapers had to be ready on Friday afternoon to be handed out to the students first thing on Monday morning. Right after the newspapers were in the students' hands, the club started creating the next edition.

"Getting a paper out on time every other week is difficult," Ms. Surovsky said. "And without articles, there is no paper."

I lowered my eyes and repeated, "I'm sorry." What else could I say? I was pretty sure she was going to fire me from the newspaper staff. I braced myself for the bad news.

"I'm going to give another student a chance to write in your spot this week," she told me. "This is a tough choice for me, Jessie, but you were supposed to have an article today."

I nodded, holding back tears. She was right to give away my space. I'd have done the same if I were in her shoes.

"Perhaps you can write a feature again in a few weeks," Ms. Surovsky said.

A few weeks!

"Okay," I managed. "Thank you."

My feet felt heavy, and my heart was like a stone as I walked into the lunchroom. I wasn't hungry. Charla and Daniel were sitting at a table. I dragged myself over to join them.

Charla looked ready to burst from excitement. "I waited to share the news."

"Tell us!" Daniel shouted. "We've been waiting for hours!"

She was about to begin when suddenly she stopped and looked at me. "What's wrong, Jessie?"

I said, "I'll tell you after. We've been waiting to hear the big news since the end of art class."

"Are you sure?" Daniel asked. "You look sad."

"I'll still be sad later," I told them. "I want to hear Charla's news now."

Charla stared at me for a heartbeat, then said, "I got a text from my mom. The police found the stolen hard drive at Gloria Scott's house today. Somehow, she really did pull off the theft in broad daylight."

I gasped. That was huge. Leona had been right to accuse Gloria Scott after all. After my visit to the manor on the day of the theft, I had told Charla's mom what I had seen. At the time, she wasn't sure if she could pin the blame on Gloria Scott, but it seemed like she had all the evidence she needed now.

"There's something else," Charla said. "My mom's law firm hired a private detective to watch Ms. Scott's house. Ever since we heard that she wanted something from the safe, my mom was worried Ms. Scott was planning another break-in."

"Glad I could help," Daniel said. I was glad too. Without his spy equipment, we wouldn't have heard Ms. Scott mention the safe.

Charla said, "The detective watching Ms. Scott's house says she never left home yesterday. Her car was in the driveway all day."

"How is that possible? Are we back to thinking she had an assistant that stole the hard drive and brought it to her?" Daniel asked. "I thought we'd given up the assistant's assistant idea."

"What if we're missing another suspect?" I mused. I was partially talking to my friends, but really I was thinking out loud. "The computer room was unlocked. Anyone could have just grabbed the hard drive if they came inside the house." The daylight timing of the theft had been bothering me. "It's a bold move to break into a house when so many people are around."

All of a sudden, it hit me. I jumped up from the table so fast I almost spilled Daniel's drink.

"Whoa!" He grabbed the cup just in time.

"We have another suspect to investigate," I said, but I didn't have time to explain. "Meet me by my locker after school." Then I ran as fast as I could from the cafeteria to Ms. Surovsky's room.

I was breathing heavy when I burst through the classroom door. "Did you give away my space in the paper?" I asked. I had a cramp in my side, as if I'd run a marathon instead of just down the hallway.

"Not yet," she said, staring at me over the top of her glasses yet again. "Why?"

"Can you hold off until tomorrow?" I asked. "Please? I think I've found a connection between Dr. Potter and our school after all."

Chapter 10

A Hidden Hobby

After school, Charla, Daniel, and I headed outside to the athletic fields, where the football team was about to start practice. Football was popular at our school, and a small crowd of people had gathered to watch the players in action.

"There he is." Daniel pointed across the turf toward the end zone. "Number eleven."

Milo Miller was in his practice jersey and shorts. We watched him toss the ball with his teammates for a few minutes before he noticed us lurking in the crowd.

Daniel waved him over.

"All those guys," Charla moaned. "They're totally obsessed with football."

I noticed that JJ from English class and the *Gabber* was wearing number nine on his jersey. He spun a football on his fingertip, showing off for the others.

"If JJ spent as much time on math as he does on football tricks," Charla said, "he'd be a rocket scientist." We watched while JJ took the spinning ball and carefully balanced it on his nose. Charla shook her head. "Forget building rockets. JJ should join the circus."

Milo gave us a wave as he walked up to us. He'd heard Charla's comment. "Everyone loves a good show," he said.

"Hmmph." Charla jumped straight to the big question. "Are you working with Gloria Scott?"

Milo assumed she was accusing him. "I heard about what happened at the manor. Do you think I stole the hard drive?" He stepped forward so he and Charla were nose to nose, inches apart.

Daniel softened the question. "You were super interested in what I knew about Ms. Scott. We wondered if you knew her."

"I know her pretty well," Milo said, stepping back from Charla. "I already told you I don't think she's the type to steal anything from the Potter family. Gloria adored Clarisse Potter."

I considered the answer. Just because Gloria Scott liked Dr. Potter and thought highly of the family didn't mean she wouldn't steal from them. "You were at the house around the time the break-in happened yesterday," I said to Milo. "I saw you there."

He nodded.

"Did you notice anything strange?" I asked.

"I was already home by the time the hard drive was stolen," he said. He looked directly at Charla as he continued, "I don't know anything about the break-in, but I think Gloria is innocent."

"I wasn't accusing you," she said.

The two of them stared at each other for what seemed like hours before Milo finally broke the silence. "Sorry, I'm a little touchy when it comes to Gloria," he said. "I'm not officially her assistant or anything, but sometimes I help her with stuff. It's a trade. I water her plants or walk her dog, and she teaches me coding."

"Coding?" said Charla. I watched her facial expression soften. With one word, it seemed like Charla's opinion of Milo had flipped. She'd thought he was just a loud football player who hung out with other loud football players, but now she knew there was more to Milo Miller. "Are you serious?"

"As serious as a network worm," he replied.

"Oh, that is serious!" Charla said. She turned to me and Daniel. "Network worms are destructive programs that can infest any linked computers."

"Grim," Daniel said, giving me a side glance. Milo was more complicated, and interesting, than any of us had realized.

"Keep it quiet though. Coding is a big secret for me," Milo whispered to us. He peeked back over his shoulder at his football friends. "My friends on the team don't know."

I looked over at JJ, who was now bouncing footballs off his forehead. The interesting thing to me was that JJ loved football and showing off, but he also wrote for the paper. And while Charla thought he was bad at math in class, I'd seen JJ calculate all kinds of sports statistics in his head.

None of us were just interested in one thing.

I liked mysteries *and* journalism.

Daniel liked painting *and* mysteries *and* theater. Well, maybe not theater. That was yet to be decided.

Charla liked computers *and* being creative.

Milo liked football *and* coding.

I was a little sad that Milo's friends didn't know he loved coding. But it was his secret, and he could share it when he was ready.

"Gloria introduced me to coding," he said. "I was mowing the lawn one day when she told me that the work I was doing was like a simple code. A computer can only do what it was asked to do and nothing else. I was asked to mow the lawn in rows, so I did. Back and forth until I ran out of lawn."

I recognized a loop like Charla had explained. "The end of the lawn is the thing that breaks the loop," I said, feeling proud of my tech knowledge.

"Exactly," Milo said with a grin. "Gloria told me that a robot could mow the lawn if we programmed it to do that." I could tell he really admired her. "Together, we started building a simple prototype."

"You were learning robotics at Dr. Potter's house?" Charla was clearly excited. "That's so awesome."

"Yeah," Milo said.

His friends had started chanting his name in an effort to get him back on the field: "Mi-lo! Mi-lo!"

"I gotta run," he told us. "But you can see why I'm so worried about Gloria." He met Charla's eyes. "You'd like her if you knew her."

"I'd like to meet her," Charla said, intrigued.

I reminded Charla that Gloria Scott was also the number-one suspect in a crime at Potter Manor and that she might be in jail soon.

"There's all kinds of drama at that manor. As long as I've been around, it's been Leona and Gideon versus Gloria," Milo said as the chanting of his name got louder. Even more of the football players were doing it now.

JJ tossed a ball at Milo. He caught it, then said, "I think the Potters are setting Gloria up." He threw the ball back to JJ, then told us, "I haven't talked to her since all this stuff began, but I think you should dig a little deeper on Leona and Gideon.

Milo started to leave but then spun around as if something had suddenly occurred to him. "Come to my house later tonight," he said. "It's near the manor. Daniel knows how to get there." He looked over his shoulder, then lowered his voice. "I've got more to tell you. But I don't want to talk about it here."

Chapter 11

Three Voices

After school, I called Grandfather. He said it was okay if I went to dinner at the Tortilla Truck with Daniel and Charla that night. The Tortilla Truck wasn't really a truck. It used to be, but it got so popular that its owners opened a real restaurant and kept the name. The old truck was parked behind the restaurant, kind of like my family's boxcar.

As we waited in line to order dinner, Daniel was in an especially good mood. I could tell because he began acting out everything he said. "Milo," he said as he imitated a football player catching a ball, "says Gloria Scott is innocent."

"Milo has football brain," Charla replied. "All the evidence points to Ms. Scott." She pretended to pound a judge's gavel. "Guilty as charged!"

Daniel pretended to have a gavel of his own. "Innocent!"

I wasn't sure either way. I took out my phone and began scrolling through my notes.

The evidence we had so far did seem to point to Gloria Scott. Plus, the police actually found the missing hard drive at her house. Then again, the video evidence didn't definitively show what Leona and Gideon Potter claimed it showed. There was no solid proof that Ms. Scott had actually been inside the manor that time and no proof she'd been there when I was visiting either. It was hard to decide a case based on half facts.

"I think Leona and Gideon could be hiding something," I said. I began to spell out a few of the strange details that I'd noted. "Why is the computer room open and the door across the hall locked? Why are they obsessed with security? Why did they make Kane seem like a killer when he is really just a silly puppy?" I had a list of questions longer than the line at the Tortilla Truck.

We ordered three classic burritos and loaded nachos to share. Charla found us a table while Daniel and I brought over the trays.

"I'm not totally convinced we can trust Milo," I said while scooping up some salsa on a tortilla chip.

"Me either," Charla agreed.

"I thought you'd trust him more now that you know he's a coder," I said before taking a big gulp of water. The salsa was superhot.

"Coders are not all trustworthy. After all, we know that someone in my club sent the video of Daniel around to the whole school," Charla said. "I'm sure you've noticed that I've been grumpy at them ever since." She bit into a nacho topped with a hot pepper, and her face started turning red. After a long drink of water, she was able to continue. "Milo keeps his coding a secret, which makes him somewhat suspicious. What kind of person would want to hide their coding abilities? Only a hacker who was up to no good. Gloria Scott started as a hacker, and maybe Milo is following in her footsteps. Hackers are rarely known to be honorable. Even when they hack for a decent cause, it's still breaking into someone else's computer. Totally illegal."

Leona Potter had said pretty much the same thing.

"I thought you liked Milo," Daniel said to Charla. "You seemed excited when you found out he's learning to code."

"I do like him," said Charla. "But that doesn't mean I believe him if he says Gloria Scott's innocent. I'll admit, I'm jealous that he's been learning robotics from Dr. Potter's right-hand woman. That's so cool." Charla dunked a chip into the salsa and shrugged. "Maybe Gloria Scott is guilty, but I could be wrong. Maybe she's not."

"Let's finish up dinner and head over to Milo's," I said. "We're not going to be able to figure anything else out until we hear what he has to say."

◦ ◦ ◦

Milo's house was next door to the manor, but it was so much smaller that it seemed almost invisible. The manor was old and big and had a lot of grass. Milo's house was new and barely had any grass to mow. The yard was cement.

"My dad doesn't have time to mow," Milo explained when he met us at the door. "I like earning extra money, so I learned to use a lawn mower at my mom's house." He gestured for us to follow him inside and offered us something to drink.

My mouth was still on fire from the spicy nachos, so I gladly accepted a glass of water. Milo brought out cookies. "My dad loves entertaining guests," he said. "We're always prepared."

I laughed. "Grandfather is like that too," I said. "But my brother Benny usually eats the cookies before anyone else gets a chance."

Milo's dad's cookies were homemade peanut butter. It was hard to keep seeing Milo as a suspect in our mystery when we were eating delicious cookies in his living room.

Charla and I sat on a low sofa. Daniel was in a rocking chair. Milo stood as he talked. He'd changed after school and was now wearing jeans and a light-colored sweater.

"Leona and Gideon fought with Gloria all the time," Milo told us. "Even before Dr. Potter died, I could hear them yelling at each other through the windows." He crossed his arms. "It got worse after the accident."

"You wear headphones when you mow," I said, stating an obvious fact. "And lawnmowers are loud."

"I started wearing the headphones so I didn't have to hear them shouting when I was doing the quieter stuff like raking leaves and trimming the edges of the yard," he explained. "It felt like I shouldn't listen to private stuff when I'm working there."

Trustworthy yet? I saw Daniel mouth to Charla. She replied with a shrug.

"What did you hear before you started wearing headphones?" I asked as I opened the notes app on my phone and started to write down Milo's answers.

"Right after Dr. Potter died," Milo said, "the three of them were arguing in the parlor."

I imagined those big windows and recalled seeing Milo working just outside them. If the doors were open and he wasn't wearing headphones, he would have definitely been able to hear everything they were saying.

"The next day, I decided to bring my headphones," Milo said.

"What did you hear?" Daniel asked.

"Gloria and Gideon Potter were screaming at each other," he said. "It was terrible." Milo paused for a moment, then said, "Gloria wanted to go to the house's library."

"Library?" I asked. "What library?" I hadn't seen that room.

"It's by the parlor," Milo said. "Gloria was upset because Gideon told her she couldn't go inside. Then he threatened that if she ever went into the library, he'd have her arrested for trespassing. He said she'd go to jail forever." A shiver went through Milo. "The way he said it was scary."

"Sounds like his threats ended up being real," Charla said. "At first, Ms. Scott was being sued because she had papers they wanted back. After that, she was accused of breaking and entering, but the judge let her go. And now she's being accused of breaking and entering again."

"And stealing the hard drive," Daniel added. "Stealing is the bigger crime."

"I think Gideon and Leona set her up," Milo said. "Or at least Gideon did."

"It sounds possible," I said. "If he threatened her before it happened."

"There's one more thing I forgot to mention," Milo said. He pulled his phone out of his back pocket. "Right after that fight, Gloria sent me a text. Usually she'd text me the times to meet up for tutoring, but this time it was just random numbers."

Milo showed us his screen. The latest message from Ms. Scott read: 324562.

"That's not a phone number," Charla commented. "Not enough digits."

"Or a calendar date," Daniel said.

"I don't know what it is," Milo said, staring at his phone. "But after this, Gloria stopped returning my texts and we stopped meeting."

I typed out everything Milo said, then studied my notes. I scrolled up to refresh my memory on some of the things that had happened recently.

On the day we'd gone to the courthouse, I'd written a note that said simply, "SAFE?" I said the word out loud.

"*Safe*? Like in baseball, when the player gets to base?" Milo asked.

"Not everything's a sport," Charla groaned. "*Safe* as in a secure box to store important papers or jewels."

"Ah," Milo said. "I should have known that. Sports are cool, but maybe I should read a few mysteries." He smiled at us.

"Good idea." Charla gave him a thumbs-up.

"I guess this means that Milo's not a suspect anymore?" Daniel asked us, loud enough for Milo to hear.

"He's safe," I said, chuckling at my own wordplay.

I had to admit, I was a little disappointed. I'd thought Milo would be my school connection to the Potter Manor mystery, but now it was clear that I had to find another link if I wanted to write this feature.

"Totally innocent," Charla echoed.

"I was a suspect?" Milo raised an eyebrow at me.

"You're the assistant's assistant," Charla told him as if that explained it.

"It's a mystery." I raised one shoulder in a half shrug.

"Everyone's a suspect until they aren't anymore."

"Whew," Milo said. "Well, now that my name is cleared, I want to help however I can. If we can prove Gloria is innocent, maybe she'll be able to teach me coding again."

Together, we laid out some of the facts from the case. When we circled back to the word *safe*, I realized what we had been missing. "I've got it!" I said. "The numbers that Ms. Scott sent to Milo could be the numbers for a combination lock."

"Six is the same number of digits as the locks on our lockers, so it makes sense," Charla said. "But where is the safe the combination will unlock? And why is it so important?"

"I have an idea where it could be," Milo told us. "The last time I met with Gloria in the manor, we walked past a room where someone was installing a tough-looking lock on the door."

I looked at Charla, and she gave me a nod. "I know just the door you're talking about," I said.

"A locked safe inside a locked room." Daniel's eyes widened. "That's some serious security."

"The Potter children are into security," I said. "Big time."

"We should check it out." Milo grabbed four flashlights from the hall closet.

"Nothing illegal, please," Charla said. "My mom would be wrecked if I got arrested."

I agreed. Daniel too. The last thing we wanted was to end up in jail for snooping.

"I promise," Milo said. "We're just looking around the manor to see what's what." He shouted, "Hey, Dad, I'm going out! Be back in a little while."

I hadn't realized Milo's father was home. A voice boomed from upstairs. "Where are you going?"

"Potter Manor," Milo said. He went there so often that going now wasn't unusual. And it was right next door, so it wasn't far enough for his dad to worry.

Mr. Miller's head appeared at the top of a long narrow stairway. It wasn't very late, but he was already dressed in a robe and slippers. "Who are you going with?" he asked.

Milo looked around at me, then Charla, and finally Daniel. His face broke into a huge grin when he said, "My new friends."

∘ ∘ ∘

I thought there was only one way into the manor property—through the main gate. But there was also a side entrance that Milo used when he came to mow. He had a key to the small iron padlock.

I looked around for a security camera but didn't see one pointed at this entry. There was no obvious little green glowing light blinking in the darkness. Perhaps Leona and Gideon were only concerned about intruders who used the front gate.

The iron entry creaked as it swung open on rusted hinges.

The house was dark. I wondered if anyone was home.

"Over there. There's a single light." Daniel showed us where a soft yellow bulb glowed through a window.

I tried to envision the inside of the house, but even though I had been there twice, I wasn't positive of the layout. Charla also wasn't sure if that light was in the parlor or some other room.

Milo asked me to point a flashlight toward a patch of dirt. "I was going to plant roses out here, but it's not the right season." He used a stick to draw a quick map of the house. "If we are looking down the hallway from inside, the parlor would be here." Milo drew an *X* in the dirt. "We'd go down this hallway." He dragged the stick across the dirt map. "And the locked room would be right here." Milo dug the stick into the ground, marking the spot.

I looked at Milo's drawing, then up at the house. "That's exactly where the light is shining."

"Nice artwork," Daniel said, complimenting him.

"Thanks," Milo said. "Not as good as the perspective drawing Jessie did though."

"You saw that?" I was glad it was dark so Milo couldn't see me blush.

"Mr. Masoud was very proud. He showed it to everyone. I have art last bell," Milo said. "I heard him say he's planning to enter it in the citywide competition."

"Ugh," I said. I knew he was going to show it around, but I hadn't realized he'd displayed my work to most of the seventh grade. And he hadn't mentioned entering it in any competitions. Double ugh.

"Jessie, no more art talk! Let's go." Charla nudged me in the back and I flicked off the flashlight.

We snuck across the yard until we were directly under the window where the light was shining. It was cracked open, and we gathered in the shadows, struggling to hear what the voices inside were saying.

"We don't have the code, and I can't see any other way of getting inside." That was Leona for sure.

"We need to...*convince* Gloria to give it to us." That was Gideon, and his words sounded threatening. "Honestly, I wasn't expecting her to resist so much. It seems like she'd rather go to jail than give us what we want."

I was about to step back from the window when I heard a third person start talking. "We're going to be fighting with her for years if we can't get ahold of the will. We need that code, and we need it now."

There were three people in the room. Who could that third one be? It was definitely a man, but the voice was much deeper than Gideon's. That was all I knew.

"Jessie, that voice is familiar," Charla whispered to me.

"I know," I whispered back. Where had we heard it before? And when?

I heard a door click open, then the light in the room went out. The area where we were standing was suddenly plunged into pitch-black darkness. I was about to flick on my flashlight so we could find our way back to the side gate when the nighttime silence was suddenly broken by the sound of Milo screaming.

Chapter 12

Connecting the Dots

A man's voice shouted out through the darkness, "Who's out there?"

There was a scuffling sound and then the thumping noise of someone running through the house.

I didn't dare move or make a sound. Charla had her hand over Daniel's mouth, and he was gripping her arm.

I looked at Milo. He was red, sweaty, and completely panicked.

"That killer dog bit me!" Milo whispered in a

frightened breath, glancing down at his side while frozen in place. "I'm going to get rabies."

I put out my hand toward the dog. Kane moved away from Milo and started licking my fingers. "Are you sure he bit you?" I asked as Kane flopped over on the ground, begging for a belly scratch. I knelt down and gave his tummy a rub.

Milo checked out his leg. "No blood." He admitted, "It might have been a nudge, instead of a bite."

"That was a pretty loud scream for a puppy nose pressed against your leg," Charla giggled.

"I thought he was evil," Milo said, staring suspiciously at the dog. "Gideon warned me to never ever open the dog kennel when I'm on the property." He bent next to me and let Kane sniff his fingers before patting the dog's head. "He said this dog would tear any intruder to shreds."

Daniel chuckled. "He must have been thinking of a different dog." Kane rolled over, then put out a paw to shake with Milo.

"Gideon basically told us the same thing," Charla told Milo. "He wanted us to be afraid."

"I was scared," I admitted, "until I came by to interview Leona and Kane greeted me at the door. This is the second-nicest dog in town." I chuckled. I couldn't put another dog over Watch.

"We know you're out there!" the man shouted again. The front porch light flicked on, flooding the lawn with a bright yellow glow.

"Our cover's blown," Daniel said, squatting low in the shadows like a secret agent on a mission. "It's time to bang and burn."

"Huh?" I asked.

"A book came with my last spy gear order. It's called *The Language of Espionage*," said Daniel. "'Bang and burn' is when a spy destroys everything while they escape. The bang is an explosion meant to distract, and the fire covers the escape tracks."

"I vote no banging or burning at the manor," Charla said. "But I'm all for escaping."

"This way." Milo started toward the side gate.

Kane whimpered. He wanted to come along.

Someone entered the yard with a flashlight and was heading in our direction.

"Go away, Kane," I said, but he kept walking along with us. I pointed at the flashlight beam. "Go there."

"Fetch!" Milo said in a voice that was a little too loud. He threw a stick across the lawn and Kane went running for it. When the coast was clear, we sprinted out the gate with Milo and didn't stop until we were safely in his living room.

Daniel gave Milo a high five. "That was awesome, the way you got him to chase the stick—good thinking!"

Milo shrugged. "I like throwing things—balls, Frisbees, sticks…"

We all collapsed together, squishing into the sofa.

"I don't think Gloria Scott was after a computer hard drive at all," I said, reviewing what we'd learned tonight. "She wants Dr. Potter's will, and it seems to be in a safe."

"A safe that's in a locked room," Charla added.

"The same safe that we might have the code for," Daniel put in.

"I've been thinking about the video evidence from your mom's computer, Charla." I leaned my head back into the sofa cushion. "There was an edit between Ms. Scott entering the house and her running away from the dog."

Charla knew exactly what I was saying. "That hall-way camera," she said. "If she'd gone into Dr. Potter's computer room, it would have recorded her."

"What if," I said, "Ms. Scott tried to get into the library instead. The camera would have shown her entering the room on the right side of the hallway instead of the left."

"They'd for sure want to edit that part out of the video," Daniel said, "and just leave the parts that they sent as evidence of the break-in."

"So Ms. Scott probably did try sneaking into the house," Charla said, her faced scrunched up in deep thought. "But she wasn't after the hard drive. She was after the will. Why wouldn't the Potters just have her arrested for trying to break in to the locked room?"

All of a sudden, it dawned on me. "Leona and Gideon don't want anyone to know about the will," I said. "They're afraid Dr. Potter left her research mate-rials to someone else. And Charla's mom told us that if there's no will, the Potters have the legal right to keep their mother's things."

As soon as I said it, we all knew it was true. Ms. Scott

wanted the will to be revealed because she thought it would give her the legal right to keep Dr. Potter's work. And the Potter siblings wanted the will to stay hidden for the exact same reason.

"Wait a second," Daniel said. "If Ms. Scott didn't steal the hard drive, who did?"

He had a good point. I thought for a moment before responding. "We know she was at home when the hard drive was stolen. Someone else could have taken it and planted it at her house."

It seemed like a long shot, but it was the only other explanation.

"Jessie," Charla said, rising up off the couch in excitement. "Where was Gideon when the lights went out that day?"

"I...don't know," I answered, realizing right away what she was getting at. "I never saw him."

"I knew it!" Milo shouted. "They *have* been trying to frame Gloria."

If our theory was right, Leona had used me to help make their framing of Ms. Scott more convincing. I felt betrayed. Leona had seemed nice, but she really just wanted me to be there when the lights went out and the hard drive went missing.

"It makes perfect sense," Daniel said. "When we were listening under the window, Gideon talked about trying to convince Ms. Scott to give up the safe code by threatening her with jail time. He took the hard drive himself and planted it at Ms. Scott's house!"

Milo's dad appeared at the top of the stairs. "There's a lot of commotion down here. Everything okay?"

"Great, Dad!" Milo said. "We just solved a crime!" He blinked, then looked back up the stairs at his dad and edited his statement. "I mean we *might* have just solved a crime," he said. "But we have to do a little more investigating."

"Sounds like a fun game," Mr. Miller said. "I'm going to bed. Milo, please lock up when your friends leave."

"Sure thing, Dad," Milo said. After his father left, he asked, "Where were we?"

I pulled out my phone and opened my notes, relieved that Milo's dad hadn't asked more questions about the investigation. "Leona and Gideon Potter claim they want all their mother's notes for a project. Gloria won't give the notes back to them, so they hire Charla's mom to sue her. Later, they accuse her of trying to steal a hard drive from the house and try to get her arrested."

"Wait a second," Charla interrupted. "There's still one thing that doesn't make sense."

"What's that?" I asked.

"The original video file," said Charla. "If Leona and Gideon are the real culprits here, why would they hack into my mom's computer? And how?"

With all of the other developments, I'd forgotten all about the event that had kicked off this mystery. "That's a good question," I said. "Leona and Gideon definitely don't have the computer skills to do something like that."

"I guess it doesn't matter right now." Charla sat back down on the couch. "The main thing seems to be that safe code. The Potters know Ms. Scott has it, so they are trying to bully her into giving it up, along with Dr. Potter's research."

"But they don't know that I have the code," Milo said. He held up his phone. "If we can somehow get to that safe, we could blow this case wide-open."

"Our main suspects are now Leona and Gideon Potter," Daniel said.

"There's another suspect too," I reminded everyone. "Don't forget a third person was also in the room with them tonight. We don't know who it was, but his voice sounded weirdly familiar to me."

"I recognized it too," Charla said. "But I've got no idea why." She yawned. "We should get going; it's late." She was right. It was a school night, and we were all tired from the excitement of sneaking onto the manor grounds.

There was one more thing I had to ask before we went though.

"Milo," I said, "I need to write an article for the next edition of the *Greenfield Gabber*. Ms. Surovsky is holding space for me. Can I write about you? Not as a suspect, but as the guy who is going to set Gloria Scott free."

"Me?" he asked. "Why me?"

"You're the school connection to this mystery at Dr. Potter's manor," I explained.

Milo considered my proposal for a few moments.

I could tell he understood what this meant. If I wrote about his connection to the manor, his secret coding hobby would be out in the open for all of his football friends to see.

At last he said, "I'll do it." He smiled. "But I have one condition."

Chapter 13

Identity Revealed

The instant school was out, Charla, Daniel, and I headed to my house to talk things over in the boxcar. Violet and Benny had been making snacks in the kitchen and offered to make some for me and my friends too.

I carried the bowl of popcorn they'd made out to the boxcar. It had cinnamon spice seasoning on it—a Benny Alden original flavor. Violet had added a cute card that said "Spice Up Your Day" to the treat.

As I rolled the clanging door shut, Daniel made a

dive for the one and only beanbag chair in the club-house. "All mine!" he exclaimed, settling in.

Charla took my desk chair, leaving me to sit on the floor.

If we kept meeting like this, we'd need more chairs. Or a couch.

Charla said, "I'm dying to talk about everything we've discovered. I think we should spill what we've learned to my mom."

I stretched my legs straight across the worn wooden floor. The boxcar was my favorite place to hang out, and being inside it made it easier for me to think.

"We need to be 100 percent sure about the details," I said. "Your mom is the lawyer accusing Gloria Scott of stealing from the Potters. If we accuse the Potters and we're wrong, it would be worse than bad."

I picked up my phone to look at my notes again.

"We have a pretty good idea of what we think happened," I said. "I wish we could review it step-by-step. Maybe if we see everything we know in action, we'd realize what's missing." Charla and I both turned our heads toward Daniel and gave him a pointed stare.

Daniel pretended not to notice us as he took a handful of popcorn. "This is delicious! Sweet and spicy at the same time." He chewed slowly and swallowed before speaking. "Oh, did you ladies need me to do something?" He smiled, then stood up. "Since I'm not trying out for the theater club, this will be my one and only performance. Let's get started."

"Which role do you want?" I asked.

"The best one," he said, rolling his eyes. "Obviously."

Charla laughed. "Which one would that be?"

"For this performance, the role of Dr. Clarisse Potter will be performed by the amazing Daniel Garza, thespian of the boxcar." He took a bow and rose with a flourish.

"But I wanted to play Dr. Potter," Charla whined.

"You get to be Kane," Daniel said, prompting Charla to give a playful bark.

"Our play opens on Dr. Potter, at home, at her desk, writing her will," Daniel said, setting the stage with a theatrical whisper. "The room looks like a bizarro cave." Then he raised his voice and imitated Dr. Potter. "I, Dr. Clarisse Potter, do hereby leave my life's work to my two children."

I stopped the show. "Three children."

"Three?" Daniel broke character. "I'm not the math wiz Charla is, but I think Leona plus Gideon equals two."

"There's a third," I told Daniel. "Charla"—I pointed at my computer—"can you find that obituary for Dr. Potter again?"

"Of course." She pulled it right up. Daniel and I stood over Charla's shoulder. I pointed. "It says three."

"Can you find out the person's name?" Daniel asked Charla.

"I'm offended you're even asking." Charla laughed. The keys clattered as she searched the web. "Mitchell Potter," she said at last. It took a bit longer, but soon, Charla had his address and his phone number and a minute later, his job.

"Hmm, it says he's a custodian at an office building downtown," Charla said. "Wait a minute. This can't be right. It says he works at my mom's building."

A split second later, we both turn to each other. "The janitor!"

"I knew that husky voice was familiar," I said.

Daniel hadn't been with us the night we'd gone to

Charla's mom's office, so we had to explain. We reminded him about the tone of the voice we'd heard while hiding outside the window of Potter Manor.

"It was the same person," I said. "The janitor at the law office is Leona and Gideon's brother."

"Are you sure?" Daniel asked.

"Positive," I said.

"What do we do now?" Daniel asked. He frowned. "Looks like my boxcar performance is canceled."

"Not canceled," I said. "Pack it up. We're going to take this show on the road."

"I'm confused," Daniel said.

"We need to go see Charla's mom," I said. "You can do the second act there."

∘ ∘ ∘

Charla's mom was in a meeting when we arrived, but she'd given us permission to wait in her office until she was done.

Mrs. Gray's laptop was on the couch, and her main desktop computer was on the desk. Charla booted up the desktop while I turned on the laptop.

"New password?" I asked Charla.

"You know it!" Charla said. "And it's not Charla-12345."

"Way to go, Mrs. Gray!" I laughed.

"My mom has a remote-access program that lets her move back and forth between her two computers," Charla explained to Daniel. "Mom can log in to one computer from the other." She took the laptop and set it next to the larger computer. "Remember what I told you, Jessie? If Mom deletes an email at home, it deletes at the office too."

"Because they both sync up with the main email server," I said. Charla smiled proudly at me.

She showed us how that worked. Charla sent her mom an email. It appeared in the mail program on both computers. Daniel and I watched the message appear on both screens, then disappear from both computers when she deleted it.

"Downloads are different," she explained. "Those files go directly to the hard drive." She made up a pretend file called "test" and attached it to an email. Then she downloaded the file onto both hard drives. Finally, she deleted the file off the desktop computer. But the test file was still on the laptop.

"I'll delete it now," Charla said. Using remote access from the desktop, she took control of the laptop and used the cursor to move the test file toward the trash.

While she was doing that, I noticed the paperweight that I'd held as a weapon the night the janitor, Mitchell Potter, appeared in the doorway and startled us. I grabbed it to show Daniel.

Just as Charla was about to permanently delete the test file from the laptop's hard drive, my arm brushed the laptop's keypad. Both computers went blank for a second, then returned as if nothing happened.

"Oh no! Sorry." I thought I'd broken Mrs. Gray's laptop. I hoped Charla could fix it, but when I looked at her, Charla had this wild look in her eyes.

"Jessie, what does that remind you of?" she asked.

I thought about it a moment, but I had no clue what she meant. I shrugged in response to her question.

"This is the same thing that happened on the night the file was deleted from my mom's laptop! It was remote access!" She turned the laptop toward me and Daniel. "The hacker took over the mouse on Mom's laptop. They were here. I was home. We struggled for a second over who had control. In the confusion, Daniel's video got emailed out to the entire coding club."

I remembered the jumping, jittery cursor and the way the screen had blinked on and off that night. "So that means the person who deleted the evidence from your mom's computer was probably Mitchell Potter," I said.

Charla looked confused. "But why would the Potters want to erase the video file? They were the ones who sent it, and it had evidence against Gloria Scott."

Daniel popped up to his feet. "The Potters needed to erase the file they'd sent to Charla's mom because it was the wrong video!"

Now I was standing too. "Gideon and Leona, or just Gideon, or just Leona, sent Charla's mom the whole video with the hallway footage!"

"It would have shown Gloria Scott wasn't interested in the hard drive." Charla got up. "She wanted the will."

"Our mysterious third suspect is Mitchell Potter," I hissed between tight lips. "The night custodian."

"Leona and Gideon's secret brother," Daniel said.

Charla shut down both computers. "We gotta tell Mom."

Just then, Mrs. Gray entered the office. She leveled her dark brown eyes at Charla. "Tell me what?"

Chapter 14

Cracking the Code

The sun was setting when we met at Potter Manor on Wednesday afternoon.

Charla's mom had called the judge and told her about the safe. The judge wanted everyone together. If the will was in the safe, everyone had to see it. So here we were, gathered in the library at Potter Manor around a tall, heavy steel box sealed with a combination lock.

Gloria Scott and her attorney stood by the judge.

Leona and Gideon were there as well, of course.

Gideon was the one who had grudgingly let us all into the library. Charla's mom stood with them.

Daniel, Charla, and I hung back while Milo entered the numbers from his phone into the keypad. He paused. "Gloria, are you sure you don't want to do the honors?"

"I trust you. That's why I send you the code. I had been hoping you'd figure it out and open the safe while you were working here. It's time to make that happen. Open the safe, Milo." Ms. Scott moved closer to her lawyer, away from the steel box. She looked to Gideon and Leona and added, "I honestly don't know what's inside. I deciphered the lock code from her journals after she died."

"And we successfully prevented *you* from stealing, destroying, or changing the will!" Gideon replied harshly. "Thank goodness Kane is such a good guard dog."

Kane, who had been dozing nearby in a fluffy dog bed, perked up his head and started to wag his tail at the sound of his name. I held back a laugh.

The only person missing from the gathering was

Mitchell Potter. I wondered what he was doing. Mrs. Gray told him to meet us all at the manor, instead of starting his work shift at her office. She hadn't heard from him since.

Dr. Potter's cave-like computer room was strange. Her library was even weirder.

Where the computer cave was built of rock, the library was like a forest. A big sculpture of a tree rose up from the center of the floor. Bookshelves were carved out of the trunk. High in the branches was a tree house that could be used as a reading room. The walls were wood paneled, the floor was wood, and the ceiling was painted like a blue sky.

Milo pointed out a cloud as it floated by. "I think that's a video projection," he said.

"Mother loved nature," Leona told us. "She said that programming kept her inside too much. She liked this house because of the big windows looking over the lawn from the parlor. But there's only one tree in the yard. Over the years, she added interior landscaping to her workspaces. Before she died, she had talked about putting a river though the parlor."

"Of course," I said as if that were totally normal.

"Mother also had an incredible collection of books about programming," Leona said. I could tell Charla was mesmerized by the titles surrounding us. Her head kept turning back and forth as she tried to take it all in.

"You're going to strain your neck," I warned.

"I'm thinking about quitting seventh grade and living here instead," she told us. "I'd read programming books all night long."

"The house is a little creepy," I said. "You wouldn't last a night."

We both knew Charla was a bit of a chicken when it came to the possibility of ghosts and haunted houses. "I'd make you and Daniel stay with me," she told me.

Daniel and I laughed, but then the room became quiet as Milo began punching the code into the safe.

"324562." Milo said the numbers out loud as he tapped them.

"We should have known," Gideon said to his sister, but we all overheard him. "Those are the jersey numbers of her favorite Greenfield Gators players. Johnson is thirty-two. Radcliff is forty-five. And Lopadopolous is sixty-two!"

"The Gators are our local minor league baseball team," Milo explained to me, Daniel, and Charla.

"Mother loved sports," Leona told us. "She wasn't *just* a computer programmer."

"She wasn't only interested in one thing," I remarked. "No one is."

I turned to see Milo grinning harder than ever before. "Sports and programming," he cheered. "A perfect combination." Just as he said the word *combination*, the lock on the safe clicked open. There was a single sheet of paper inside.

"Please let it say she left everything to us," Gideon said to no one in particular.

Leona crossed her fingers. "Nothing can happen unless we have permission, free and clear, from my mom."

"If you were so sure the will would give you the rights to all her work, you wouldn't have framed me," Gloria said.

"We didn't frame you," Leona Potter countered.

"Everyone in town already thought you were involved in mother's car accident. There were rumors. We just never countered the gossip. We let everyone believe what they wanted."

"You accused me of stealing Dr. Potter's notes!" Gloria said, her voice rising in anger. "You knew she wanted me to have them. She said so right in front of you." She added, "You and Gideon think you're so sneaky, but Clarisse knew all along that you'd sell her life's work as soon as she was gone."

"Mother didn't understand the value of what she'd created," Gideon said. "Once her will makes it clear that we own Mother's work, we'll finally use it to make as much money as she deserved."

"We'll soon find out who owns the notes, the hard drive, and everything else." The judge stood in the center of us all, by the bookcase tree. She studied the page. "We have a problem though…I'm not sure what this means." She rubbed her eyes and looked again. "It's strange. Is it a foreign language?"

The judge held up the page so we could all see what was typed on it.

```
var attendance = prompt("How many people
   are here?");
if (parseInt(attendance) < 5) {
   Beneficiary = "Gloria";
} else if (parseInt(attendance) < 10) {
   Beneficiary = "GLS";
} else {
   Beneficiary = "Ms. Scott";
}
```

Charla laughed. "Of course it's written in computer code," she said.

"Mother!" Leona shook her fist as if her mother's ghost was in the room. "Even after you die, you're still mad that Gideon and I never learned to code?"

"She's torturing us from beyond the grave," Gideon muttered with a loud groan.

"My, what an odd will," Mrs. Gray remarked. "In all my years as a lawyer, I've never seen anything like this."

"It's not *that* odd," Charla told her mom. "The will says exactly what Dr. Potter wanted to do with her estate."

"Go on," Gloria encouraged her. She obviously knew what the code meant and wanted the students to figure it out. "Let's see what Charla and Milo can tell us."

Charla reviewed the will and said, "It's a classic if/else statement."

"That means if the first condition in the statement is met, then something happens." Milo asked the judge if he could hold the will. She handed it over, and Milo added, "If the condition is *not* met, the computer moves on to the next line of code."

"Dr. Potter's if/else statement works according to the number of people present at the reading of her will," Charla said. "There are eight people here."

"Get on with it," Gideon said impatiently. "Just tell us who gets the documents."

"Let Charla and Milo reason it out," Gloria said. "Your mother was an amazing programmer, and this is her final statement."

Milo scratched his head. "If there are less than five people here, the beneficiary is Gloria."

"There are eight here right now!" Leona shrieked. "It must be us!"

Gideon was very excited. "This is terrific news." He pulled out his cell phone. "I have a call to make."

"Slow your roll, Gideon. There's more," Gloria said. "What's the next part?"

"If there are fewer than ten people here, GLS is the beneficiary," Charla said. "That means GLS is the beneficiary for attendance between five and ten people."

"Still must be us!" Leona said. "G for Gideon... L for Leona..."

"Who's the S?" Gideon asked his sister.

"Hi." Gloria raised her hand. "I'm Gloria Loraine Scott. Initials: GLS."

"Impossible." Gideon stomped his foot. "Who would leave their estate, all their belongings, to their assistant over their children?"

"Is that the final decision?" Leona asked. "Please let there be more. It would be unbelievable to base everything on how many people were around when the will was read."

Charla said, "There's one more line."

"The last part tells us that if the beneficiary is not Gloria, or GLS," Milo translated, "it will be Ms. Scott."

"How is that possible? All three—Gloria, GLS, and Ms. Scott—are the same person!" Gideon demanded they read the will again.

"It seems that no matter how many people came today, Gloria Loraine Scott is the beneficiary," the judge said.

"Dr. Potter had a sense of humor," Daniel remarked. "It's a funny will."

The judge made a proclamation. "This is the official will and testament. Dr. Potter's wishes are binding. Gloria L. Scott receives everything Dr. Potter has left behind."

"Everything?" Leona asked. She looked as though she might faint.

"The papers? The hard drive? *And* the house?" Gideon was even paler than his sister.

"Everything," the judge declared.

"Am I too late?" a raspy voice came from the library doorway. The man who entered filled the entire frame, and this time I recognized him right away.

Mitchell Potter looked at his brother and sister. "So, are we rich or what?"

"No." Gideon's shoulders slumped.

Leona stared at the floor, avoiding her younger brother's eyes.

"I took a job as a janitor for nothing!" Mitchell's voice boomed through the library. "You promised I'd be part of the new business." He was furious, and I stepped back as he stomped into the library and up to his siblings. "The sale is ruined and it's all your fault."

"Sale?" I asked. "What do you mean?"

"Last year, we were approached by a large company that wanted to buy our mother's program," Mitchell said.

"Dr. Potter refused the offer," Ms. Scott explained.

"After Mother died, we contacted the company again," said Gideon. "They're still interested. We need all notes, drives, and permission, as beneficiaries of the will, so we can complete the sale."

"Millions of dollars!" Mitchell's face was flushed. "You said I'd get a third if I helped you!" He pointed his finger at his brother and sister. "I didn't know what I was doing, but I even deleted that computer file just like you told me to."

"Mitchell made a mess of things when he tried to

delete the file," said Charla. She turned to face Mitchell Potter. "Sorry, but you're a terrible hacker."

"I know," Mitchell admitted with a shrug. "My mom always told me that too."

Gloria lowered her eyes toward Leona and Gideon. "Dr. Potter wanted her program to be open-source. That means anyone would be able to use it for free or make their own improvements and create new versions. Would you really have sold it to a private company against her wishes?"

Leona sneered. "Didn't you hear what Mitchell said? That program is worth millions of dollars. You think we should give it away for free?"

"It's what your mom wanted," Gloria said. "She wanted to protect private data from hackers. She believed everyone should be able to use her program. She was a great person, and she wanted to help as many people as she could."

"She was a batty lady who spent all her money bringing weird decorations into the house," Gideon said, knocking his fist against the library tree.

"Dr. Potter wanted a workspace that made her

happy," Daniel countered. "She worked a lot. She liked the outdoors. You should have encouraged her to have a bird sanctuary and a butterfly farm in here if that would have brought her joy."

"She did mention a petting zoo…" Mitchell Potter noted.

I was sorry I hadn't met Clarisse Potter. She sounded eccentric, smart, and wonderful. I snapped a photo of the tree in the library. Maybe Mrs. Surovsky would print it with my article.

The judge turned to Leona, Gideon, and Mitchell. "You'll need to turn over all documents, notes, papers, hard drives, and anything else you might have copied from your mother's estate. And give me the keys to the house too."

"Millions of dollars," Mitchell muttered. "Millions of dollars. Millions of dollars…"

"I think he might be stuck in a loop," I whispered to Charla.

"You're going to need a new job," Charla's mom told Mitchell. "When the building manager learns what you've done, you'll be out of work."

Mitchell grunted. "I need a lawyer."

"Good luck finding one." Mrs. Gray shook her head. "You both need a new lawyer too," she told Leona and Gideon. "I quit."

Daniel pretended to slam an invisible judge's gavel. "Case closed!"

Chapter 15

Between Friends

On Monday morning, the *Greenfield Gabber* was passed out to students as they entered school. Charla immediately flipped to the second page and found my article.

I was proud of the headline: "Football Player's Coding Talent Helps Save Clarisse Potter's Legacy."

Nine words!

I'd wanted to add a part about how he'd cleared the reputation of an innocent woman, but it didn't work in my headline. Anyone who read the article would know the whole story. The headline was exactly what it was meant to be: a starting place to get people to read the rest.

Today, Charla was wearing a shirt that said "Program with Potter" on it, in honor of my article. "Good work, Jessie!" she gushed, waving the paper. "This feature is your best yet."

I knew my *Gabber* headline had been effective when I heard students talking about Dr. Potter in the hallway. They were interested in the cybersecurity program she'd created and curious about the strange house she'd lived in. There was a lot of buzz about the tree in the library, and I was glad I had taken the photo.

Gloria Scott had told us she was thinking about opening the manor to the public after the news settled down. I hoped she'd do it. I also hoped she'd charge a few dollars for admission so she could someday install the river that Dr. Potter had wanted in the parlor.

Milo and Daniel came into school together. I'd given Milo a draft of the article for his approval. He was the connection to Dr. Potter that I'd needed to write my article. More importantly, I'd revealed his secret to the entire school.

"Make way for the celebrity," Daniel said, pushing into a narrow space between me and Charla. "Autographs are fifty cents."

"I don't need any more fame," Milo said. "The article has been out for five minutes and I've already been asked if I can make an app for the football team. My dad wants help with a programming project for work. And the coding club wants me to join."

"Yay!" Charla said, though we all knew he'd turn down the offer. Milo would rather keep studying with Gloria Scott. He had invited Charla to come along, but she'd made up with the kids at the school coding club and was sticking with them.

However, Charla planned to apply for the all-new Double-Doctor Clarisse Potter Memorial Mentorship Program over winter vacation. Gloria Scott wanted to preserve Dr. Potter's legacy in a way Dr. Potter would have loved: by teaching kids computer programming. Milo said he was going to apply too.

Obviously, Charla had suggested the program's name.

"I'll be managing Milo's career," Daniel said, "now that he's famous."

"And I'll be managing Daniel's acting career," Milo said.

"Oh, about that," Daniel said, drawing out the words. "I changed my mind. There's no acting happening."

Milo spun toward me. "Jessie! You promised! You said if I let you tell everyone about my coding skills, you'd convince Daniel to try out for the play." He pointed to a flyer posted on the hallway wall. "Auditions are today."

We had it all arranged. Charla was skipping coding, I was missing newspaper, and Milo had planned to leave football early so we could all support Daniel.

Daniel said, "Sorry, guys. I told my parents I'd help in the art shop after school instead."

"Daniel?" I said. "I thought we had a deal."

I turned to Milo. "He said he'd try out, but then Daniel made the deal more complicated. He said that *I* had to do something for *him*."

It was a deal-o-rama. Milo would do something for me if Daniel auditioned. Daniel would only audition if I did something for him.

Charla was happy to be left out of all the dealing.

"Well, did you do what I asked?" Daniel raised an eyebrow.

I reached into my backpack and pulled out an envelope. I held it toward him but refused to let go. "Are you going to be in the auditorium at 3:30?"

He snagged the envelope from my hand. "Wouldn't miss it for the world."

The bell rang and we needed to go to class.

Milo said, "See y'all later."

Daniel hurried down the hall while Charla and I took our time following behind him. When we entered the art room, Daniel held up the torn envelope. He had the pages I'd given him spread across his desk.

"You didn't tell me what you had to do for Daniel," Charla said, trying to see what he was reading.

"You should wear your glasses," I said. "You'll never see the words from here."

"I'm going to need you to investigate the case of Charla's missing glasses," she said. "I can never find those thing."

I put my hands on my head as if I were concentrating as hard as I could. "They're still on your desk, where

I saw them last," I said.

"Another case closed." Charla giggled, then squinted at Daniel. "Look at his feet. It looks like he's hopping his toes around as he reads." She looked at me and smiled. "You wrote a Hop-Man play, didn't you?"

I smiled. "That was Daniel's side of the deal-o-rama. He agreed to audition today, but only if I wrote a Hop-Man play."

Charla got a glint in her eye and grinned. "Maybe he'll make a video of himself performing. Then he can email me the video, and I'll forward it to you—"

"Whoa." I held up my hands and laughed. "No more forwarding videos."

◦ ◦ ◦

The auditions were held in the school auditorium. Milo, Charla, and I sat in the front row. If we wanted the outgoing version of Daniel we all knew outside of school, we thought it would be helpful if he could pretend we were hanging out together.

Before he went onstage, I told him, "Imagine we're in the boxcar."

"Okay." He nodded, but he looked like he might make a run for the emergency exit at the back of the room.

When Daniel came onstage, I took Charla's hand and squeezed it.

A light shone on Daniel, and he looked greener than he had in the Hop-Man video.

I heard a few giggles behind us, and a girl shouted, "Hop away!"

Daniel turned even greener.

Milo whispered to me, "I hope he doesn't puke."

"Me too," I whispered back. If the Hop-Man video was embarrassing, throwing up on the school stage would be worse.

The theater teacher, Mrs. Delgado, was also the science teacher. She gave the cue to begin, but instead of performing, Daniel started coughing. I squeezed Charla's hand so tightly that I was sure her fingers hurt.

Daniel took a sip of water. His coughing fit ended. The room fell silent. He took off his jacket. Underneath, he was wearing a custom T-shirt from Charla that said "If you liked my Hop-Man video, you're going to love this."

I held back a laugh and whispered to Charla, "That's your best shirt yet."

"I didn't really think he'd wear it." Charla grinned.

Daniel Garza stepped into the spotlight. He took a big, deep breath and the audition began…

BREAKING NEWS
There's more to the story...

Find out how Jessie, Charla, and Daniel
made headlines for the first time!

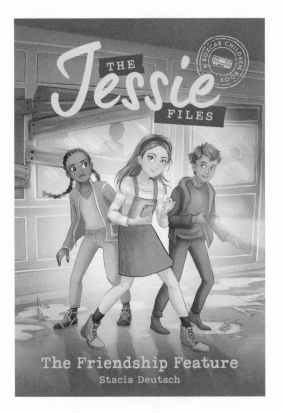

The Friendship Feature
978-0-8075-3786-2 • US $17.99

Books 3 & 4 coming Fall 2022 and Spring 2023